Praise for

DAVID ROSENFE[LT]
ANDY CARPENT[ER]

T0009195

"One of the most unforgettable authors in the genre."
—Associated Press

"Fans of legal thrillers and golden retrievers, take heart."
—*The Seattle Times*

"Reading the Andy Carpenter series by David Rosenfelt is dangerous. The books should come with warnings: 'Read with Caution,
Extremely Addicting.'" —*HuffPost*

"You should read them all." —*St. Louis Post-Dispatch*

"Without getting too sentimental or cutesy, the Andy Carpenter
novels show how our bonds with dogs can change our lives."
—*Mystery Scene*

"Rosenfelt's mysteries are always delightful reading."
—*Jersey's Best*

"For twists and turns, a story you can't put down, and dogs,
Rosenfelt's books fill the bill."
—*Kings River Life Magazine*

"This long-running series remains as fresh as ever."
—*Publishers Weekly*

"[Andy Carpenter] is probably as close to Lord Peter Wimsey as
the modern American crime genre can get." —*Booklist*

ALSO BY DAVID ROSENFELT

FLOP DEAD
GORGEOUS

David Rosenfelt

MINOTAUR BOOKS

NEW YORK

This is a work of fiction. All of the characters, organizations,
and events portrayed in this novel are either products of the author's
imagination or are used fictitiously.

Published in the United States by Minotaur Books,
an imprint of St. Martin's Publishing Group

FLOP DEAD GORGEOUS. Copyright © 2023 by Tara Productions, Inc.
All rights reserved. Printed in the United States of America.
For information, address St. Martin's Publishing Group,
120 Broadway, New York, NY 10271.

www.minotaurbooks.com

The Library of Congress has cataloged the hardcover edition as follows:

Names: Rosenfelt, David, author.
Title: Flop dead gorgeous / David Rosenfelt.
Description: First edition. | New York : Minotaur Books, 2023.
Identifiers: LCCN 2023009378 | ISBN 9781250828903
    (hardcover) | ISBN 9781250828910 (ebook)
Subjects: LCSH: Carpenter, Andy (Fictitious character)—Fiction. |
    Dogs—Fiction. | LCGFT: Detective and mystery fiction. |
    Novels.
Classification: LCC PS3618.O838 F64 2023 | DDC 813/.6—dc23/
    eng/20230307
LC record available at https://lccn.loc.gov/2023009378

ISBN 978-1-250-82892-7 (trade paperback)

Our books may be purchased in bulk for promotional, educational,
or business use. Please contact your local bookseller or the Macmillan
Corporate and Premium Sales Department at 1-800-221-7945, extension
5442, or by email at MacmillanSpecialMarkets@macmillan.com.

First Minotaur Books Trade Paperback Edition: 2024

10 9 8 7 6 5 4 3 2 1

It was at the time that Larry Hoffman started to get very rich that he started to drink.

Larry had always been a drinker to a degree; he might have one during lunch, or two during dinner. That was quite literally part of the job.

But the excessive drinking started when the money began coming in, and that was no coincidence, because that's when he started feeling the pressure.

As a managing director at Causeway Capital, an asset manager and hedge fund with more than $25 billion, it's not like Hoffman was starving. But the day he got one particular phone call, which led to one particular meeting, everything changed.

His income almost tripled literally overnight, and the effect was even greater than that because he was not paying taxes on the new money. When money comes from the places and people that Hoffman was dealing with, you don't mention it to your accountant.

There wasn't a day that went by that Hoffman wasn't sorry he went down that path. The money was incredible and intoxicating, but the fear of detection, and of so much else, didn't make it worthwhile.

It was also ruining his relationship with his fiancée; he could tell that his ever-present fear was slowly driving her away. And added to his panic was the knowledge that if everything fell apart, it could bring her down as well. She was a lawyer, and guilt by this kind of association could be career killing.

He wanted to get out, but didn't want to give up the money. Then the desire to get out became overpowering, which led to a horrifying realization.

He no longer had the option of getting out.

So that led to other decisions, and those led to more fear, which led to more drinking. Hoffman didn't think it was noticeable to his work colleagues; maybe he had one more drink than usual at lunches and dinners, but so did some of them. His fiancée knew; he was sure of that.

He lived alone, so there was no one there to watch him polish off bottles each night. And he would go to bars in the city where no one he knew hung out, and he drank quietly and alone.

Hoffman even switched bars nightly. There were so many of them on Second Avenue that he could go to a different one each night for weeks without ever having to return to one. He liked to keep it as close as he could to the Eighties, since he lived at Eighty-fourth Street and York Avenue.

It was an easy walk home, even when Hoffman wasn't in great walking condition.

On this particular night Hoffman was drinking at Monahan's, at Eighty-sixth and Second Avenue. He liked the place, because it was dark and comparatively quiet. He could sit and drink anonymously, and think about what it was he had to do.

By the fourth or fifth drink, the fear and panic would start to abate, and he could believe he had the guts to move forward. In terms of his state of mind, sobriety was the enemy.

At ten thirty, Hoffman left the bar and started walking home. He walked east along Eighty-sixth toward York. Even in his intoxicated state, he walked without staggering; no one who saw him would realize how drunk he was. He thought his doorman could tell, but was discreet enough not to say anything, except possibly to his fellow doormen.

Like every other night, Hoffman obeyed the electric signs signaling when pedestrians had the right of way to cross the street. No sense taking chances. So he did have the sign in his favor when crossing First Avenue at Eighty-sixth.

Perhaps if he were sober he would have reacted before the speeding car hit him, sending him flying more than thirty feet before landing on a parked car. The car then continued heading down the avenue at high speed, turning left and working its way toward the FDR Drive and vehicular anonymity.

Larry Hoffman was dead before his body landed on the car.

I dated Jenny Nichols in high school.

That's something I haven't mentioned a lot over the years, mainly because there was no reason to. We only had a few dates, she decided that was a few too many, and she started going out with someone else. It was fairly typical of my high school romantic life. My relationships started slow and then faded.

But once her Eastside High School days were over, Jenny followed a dream and became an actress, and about two years ago she got the lead role in a hit movie and immediately became a major star. She is both beautiful and talented, and the world seemed to discover those facts all at once. Even though she was living in Los Angeles, she became the pride of Paterson, New Jersey, where she and I grew up, and where I still live.

So, suddenly and coincidentally, I began mentioning our dating history. It's not that easy to work into a conversation without looking like a name-dropper, and early on I was a little clumsy about it.

For example, one day I was in the local delicatessen and I said, "Give me a pound of corned beef."

"Anything else?" the guy asked.

"You mean besides the fact that I dated Jenny Nichols in high school?"

I have yet another connection to Jenny, though it's not as cool as the dating thing. She was here about a year ago to visit her ailing mother in Englewood Cliffs; Jenny had bought her a home there. She must have heard that I, along with my partner, Willie Miller, run a dog rescue foundation. It's called the Tara Foundation, named after my extraordinarily wonderful golden retriever.

Jenny was anxious to adopt a dog, so she came down to the foundation and fell in love with Mamie, a seven-year-old miniature French poodle. Mamie had been turned in to the foundation when her owner died and her family had no interest in taking care of her.

Personally, if I had a family like that, I would rather spend my life surrounded by strangers.

Jenny stepped in and took Mamie back to California with her, and from that point on they seemed to be inseparable. Mamie made it to just about every magazine cover that Jenny was on, and she was on a lot of them.

As with all beautiful actresses, there is huge media speculation and reporting on Jenny's love life. I sometimes notice it when I see a story on a magazine cover at the supermarket, but I'm not that interested.

I'll occasionally skim through them, but to my knowledge they have yet to mention the fact that she dated Andy Carpenter in high school. It's a sad commentary on the state of American journalism that no reporter has dug out that fact, especially since I would be willing to give interviews.

While Jenny was here last year, my wife, Laurie Collins, and I had her and the newly adopted Mamie over for dinner. Laurie has absolutely no jealousy about Jenny, nor should she. For one thing, she trusts me.

For another, she does not have to take a back seat to anyone, in any way, and I'm including physical beauty in that. Let's put it this way: if Laurie and Jenny were ever competing in a beauty contest, Jenny would have to settle for Miss Congeniality.

We saw Jenny again about five months ago. Her mother had died, and Jenny was in town for the funeral. I personally had never seen paparazzi cover a funeral before, and it was pretty annoying. I've had my share of publicity because of some high-profile cases that I've handled, but it pales in comparison to the attention that Jenny gets.

Right now Jenny is in New York shooting a movie, and she has taken elaborate measures to evade the spotlight. The word has gone out that she's living in a midtown hotel, the Michelangelo, on Fifty-first Street. To maintain the ruse, she's even gone in there a few times, only to be shuttled out the back door by a helpful bellman named Henry.

The cloak and dagger aspect of it all, in my view, is a little over the top. Jenny's personal assistant, on the current film and previous films, is Linda Ivers. She has been in charge of keeping the media hordes away from Jenny, and Jenny says she is great at it.

In fact, according to Jenny, Linda is amazingly resourceful, can get anything done, and loves doing it.

The truth is that Jenny is actually staying in her mother's home in Englewood Cliffs, and using the opportunity to go through her things and get the house ready to be sold. The media is so far unaware of this, and Jenny has been able to stay there in total anonymity.

Tonight Laurie and I are having dinner with her again, this time at my all-time favorite restaurant, Charlie's Sports Bar, in Paterson. We've taken the private upstairs room, so hopefully the word will not get out that Jenny is there.

A bunch of our friends wanted to meet her, and Jenny was fine with that, so we've made it a small party, with everyone sworn to secrecy about her attendance. Laurie and I offered to pick her up, but Jenny declined and said she would meet us here. She's going to call when she's close, and we'll come down and bring her up through the back entrance, so she won't be seen.

At the dinner, besides Laurie and me, are Corey Douglas and his girlfriend, Dani Kendall, Marcus Clark and his wife, Julie, and my foundation partner, Willie Miller, with his wife, Sondra. Also here are Sam Willis, who serves as both my accountant and our cyber investigator, and Vince Sanders, the editor of the local newspaper and one of my sports bar buddies.

I told Vince about the party and in the process extracted a promise that there would not be a word about it in his paper. Even if I hadn't told him about it, he would have found out—he has an incredible nose for free food.

Another reason Vince is here is because I don't think he really believes that I dated Jenny in high school, even though I've probably mentioned it to him about four or five thousand times. He wants to see for himself, and thereby retain the right to mock me if it turns out that I was bullshitting.

We've only been here for about fifteen minutes when my cell phone rings. "I'm parked out front," Jenny says.

I smile at Vince as I say, "I'll be right down."

Twenty-five minutes into what passes at Charlie's for a dinner party, it's going really well.

Everybody is having a good time, and that seems to include Jenny. She's been laughing a lot, and though her phone rings a couple of times, she ignores the calls and finally powers it off.

She obviously wants to leave the real world of her career behind for a while, and she actually says something about how nice it is to spend time with normal people.

That would be us.

Vince has so far held his drooling down to a minimum, which is a pleasant surprise. Laurie and Jenny have rekindled an easy and clearly obvious friendship, even though their backgrounds and current life are very different.

Laurie is a former cop in the Paterson Police Department and part of a private investigative team with Corey and Marcus. Jenny's life is far more glamorous, but you would never know the difference watching them interact. They just seem to click together.

Of course, I am a connection between them. I'm not sure if I mentioned this, but I dated Jenny in high school.

Jenny, Laurie, Willie, and I are sitting at a table and are about to order food when the door opens. I notice Jenny react to it, and I look over and immediately recognize the person who has entered. His name is Ryan Griffin, and he is a famous actor in his own right.

He's not Jenny's level of famous but is well-known, and he is costarring with her in the film they're shooting in New York. There have been publicity stories about them dating, but I cannot confirm that one way or the other. I don't really know anything about Jenny's personal life, other than that she and I were something of an item in high school.

Griffin does not look happy, and his eyes scan the room until he finds Jenny, and he strides toward us. He's also not alone; there are two large guys in tight-fitting suits with him who look like security/bouncer types. They walk toward us also, but stay about five feet behind Griffin.

"What are you doing here, Ryan?" Jenny asks in a challenging way, clearly not happy to see him.

"I was about to ask you the same thing," he says, a fake smile on his face. "I thought we were having dinner together tonight."

"You thought wrong. I'm having dinner with friends."

"You were supposed to have dinner with me," he says, not really advancing the conversation any. The smile has already left his face; this does not seem to be a pleasant or innocent dating mix-up.

"I told you that I was not interested," she says. "You need to learn when to take *no* for an answer, Ryan. Because if you keep bothering me you're going to be hearing it a lot."

Apparently he's not in the mood to learn, because he says, "We can discuss this later, when we're alone. Let's go." It's not a request; it's more in the form of a demand.

"I'm not going anywhere," Jenny says. Even in high school she was not the type to be pushed around.

"You're going with me," Griffin says.

As the host, it seems time for me to intervene, even though I'm not anxious to. I've never been much of an intervener. "No, she isn't," I say. "She's going to stay and finish her dinner, but it's time for you to leave."

"You shut your mouth and mind your own business," he says to me, not the first person to voice those sentiments. My mouth has a tendency to get me in trouble.

Then he says, "Come on," and goes to grab Jenny's arm.

Big mistake.

Laurie is the first one to react. As Griffin reaches out and touches Jenny's arm, Laurie stands and grabs it, twisting it to the point where he goes down to the table, face first. He doesn't smash into it, but screams in pain at what Laurie is doing to his arm. It is not designed to bend in the direction that she is bending it.

The security guys react quickly and move toward the table.

Big mistake number two.

Willie, who is a black belt in karate and an all-around dangerous guy, stands up and chops one of them on the side of the head, sending him moaning to the floor. The second security guy moves toward Willie.

Mistakes come in threes.

Marcus Clark, who has been across the room, grabs the second guy from behind by the collar. Marcus, it should be noted, is the scariest, most dangerous human currently inhabiting this planet. He makes Willie look like a feeble weakling.

Marcus literally lifts the guy by the collar and throws him against the wall, headfirst. The wall seems to win the confrontation, and the guy joins his colleague on the floor.

"Come on, let go!" Griffin pleads, as Laurie has continued to twist his arm. Laurie seems unmoved by his begging.

"Please let him go," Jenny says, so Laurie does.

"Like Andy said, it's time for you to leave now," Laurie says.

"And take your two asshole friends with you." Laurie, in case you haven't figured it out yet, has no competition as the toughest person in our family.

At this point the security guys are slowly getting to their feet, with Marcus and Willie facing them to make sure they don't cause any further trouble. Remarkably, neither seems to be bleeding; their skin must be made of linoleum.

If I know Marcus and Willie, they would like another shot at them. But the three intruders seem to have left behind their trouble-causing intentions, including Griffin. I can just imagine how surprised they all are; Laurie, Willie, and Marcus are not the kind of people they would have expected to run into at a social gathering. You can walk down a lot of red carpets and never meet three people that tough.

So they seem quite willing to obey Laurie's instruction to leave, and they do so. Griffin turns and gives a sneer, which I assume is meant to be face saving, but comes off as pathetic.

Laurie, Marcus, and Willie have acted to avert what could have been an ugly scene. As is usually the case in situations like this, the part of chickenshit, inactive bystander was played by Andy Carpenter. By now I am typecast in that role.

"You okay?" I ask Jenny.

She nods, a little shakily. "I'm alright. Thank you, everyone; I'm sorry to have created a scene like that. I appreciate what you all did."

"You didn't create it," Laurie says. "He did."

"You want to talk about this and what might be going on?" I ask. "Maybe we can help."

"I really don't, Andy. Can we just have our dinner and relax?"

"If he bothers you again—" Laurie starts, but Jenny interrupts.

"I can handle him, Laurie. This isn't the first time this has happened." Then, in a brief flash of anger, "Damn him."

Vince has had his mouth open in shock at what has just transpired, and I am sure he's dying at the realization that he can't publish a recounting of it in his newspaper. But he promised that he'd keep the dinner a secret, and I have no doubt that he'll keep his word, much as he'd like not to.

"Okay," Laurie says. "But we are here and ready if you need us."

"Thank you," Jenny says. "You're all amazing."

The ringing phone wakes me up at two forty-five in the morning.

When a call comes in at that hour, the best thing that one can hope for is a wrong number. No one calls in the middle of the night to tell you that you won the lottery, or that you got a promotion.

"Andy, it's Jenny. I'm sorry to wake you."

"Is something wrong?"

"Something is very wrong. I need help. Ryan is dead; he's been murdered."

"Ryan Griffin?" I ask, a stupid question, since I doubt she means Ryan O'Neal or Ryan Seacrest or Meg Ryan.

"Yes. He was stabbed to death. The police are here."

This is not exactly computing for me, maybe because I'm not fully awake. "Where are you?"

"At my mother's house."

"And where is he?"

"Downstairs in the kitchen. I know it's a lot to ask, but can you come here? The police are scaring me."

There are a lot of other questions that I need to ask to get an understanding of what is going on, but I decide to ask them in person when I get to her house.

"I'll be there in a half hour. Don't say anything to anybody." I say this even though I have no reason to believe that Jenny might be a suspect. I don't know what's going on, but not talking to the police at a murder scene is Lawyering 101.

Apparently Jenny never took that course because she says, "I answered their questions, Andy. I didn't see any harm in it; I haven't done anything wrong. I'm sorry, I . . ."

"That's okay, Jenny. It will be fine. Just don't say anything else until I get there."

"What's going on?" Laurie asks, as I get off the phone and stand to start getting dressed. She's heard only my side of the conversation, so I fill her in on the rest.

Laurie wants to come with me, but she can't. Our son Ricky is thirteen, and while he no longer needs a babysitter when we go out, this is a different case. If he should wake up while we're gone, he might get scared at discovering that the house is empty, when we hadn't alerted him to the possibility.

I promise Laurie that I will call and let her know what's going on, and I finish getting dressed and head out. It's about a twenty-five-minute drive with no traffic, and Route 4 will be empty at this hour.

It does me no good to think about what might have happened at Jenny's, but I can't help doing so anyway. Jenny and Griffin argued tonight, in front of several witnesses, and he wound up dead at her house a few hours later. Those are two facts that, when taken together, are concerning.

She didn't say anything about killing him in self-defense over the phone, so I'm assuming her position is that she had no involvement in his death. Unfortunately, the body is in her house, so I hope she has some exculpatory information to present.

The house is on a large piece of property, set back from the street, and the nearest neighbor is quite far away. There are no streetlights; the residents must think it detracts from the ambiance. In that case, the ambiance is taking a major hit right now because the entire neighborhood seems lit up by lights from the police cars.

I pull up as close as I can and get out. As I reach the police cars, an officer comes over to me and asks where I think I'm going.

"To see my client," I say. Technically, of course, that's not true. I'm Jenny's friend, not her lawyer, but as just a friend I'd get kicked out of here.

Before he can answer, I hear, "Andy? I'm over here."

Jenny is sitting in the back of a police car, with the door open. Mamie is in her lap. "Why are you in there?" I ask.

"The detective told me I needed to leave the house and could wait in this car."

I nod. "Come with me."

She gets out of the car and an officer standing nearby says, "Hey, where are you going?"

I answer the question with one of my own. "Is she in custody?" I ask.

"No."

"Then it's none of your business where she's going."

Jenny follows me off to the side where we can talk without being overheard. She's still holding Mamie. "Tell me what happened," I say, softly.

"I really don't know, Andy. I came back after the dinner and was really tired, so I went right to bed. Mamie was acting strangely; she was barking and seemed excited, which is unusual for her. But I took her upstairs and went to sleep."

"When did Griffin come over?"

"I don't know that either. During the night Mamie started barking again, so I came downstairs to get her a chewy; I thought it might calm her down. I came down to the kitchen, and when

I turned on the light I saw Ryan lying there. There was blood everywhere."

"Had he been shot?"

"No, he was lying on his side; I saw a knife in his back." Then, "It was horrible."

"So he might have already been there when you got home?"

She nods. "I guess so. I hadn't gone in the kitchen, and maybe that's why Mamie was acting so strangely. And I didn't hear any noise from downstairs."

"What did you do after you found him?"

"I felt his neck for a pulse, but there wasn't any. He was cold, Andy, so I guess he was there for a while." Then she repeats the obvious. "It was horrible."

"Did you get blood on yourself?"

"Yes, a little bit. I washed it off while I was waiting for the police. I called nine-one-one."

"What kind of questions did they ask you?"

"Just about what happened, and if I knew him, what our relationship was . . . that kind of thing."

"Well, look who's here." The voice belongs to Captain Richard Jansing, a homicide detective with the New Jersey State Police. I've tangled with Jansing in the past, and it's fair to say that he is near the top of a very long list of police officers who somehow have remained immune to my charm.

He continues, "Let me guess. You were out chasing ambulances and stopped when you saw the lights."

I ignore the insult; not the easiest thing for me to do. But I want to get Jenny out of here. "Is Ms. Nichols free to go?"

"We're going to want to talk with her."

"At some point I might give a shit about what you want. She'll be staying at my house, in case you're hoping to get an autograph."

He smiles, unintimidated. "We'll be speaking soon, Counselor."

I return the smile. "Always a treat chatting with you, Detective." I turn to Jenny. "Come on; we'll take my car."

J enny and I didn't talk much on the way to my house last
night.

I'm sure she knows that she is potentially in legal trouble; the
police's attitudes last night would have made that clear. Plus,
the fact that someone she knew and argued with had wound up
dead in her kitchen with a knife in his back is a somewhat sus-
picious fact, and she must be aware of that.

I'd called ahead and Laurie had prepared a guest room for
her, and we all went straight to bed. While we were sleeping,
the media world exploded. Griffin's murder is the number-one,
-two, and -three story on every newscast and website, and Jenny
is already being referred to as a *person of interest*.

A bunch of the details reported are correct, including the fact
that Griffin was killed at the house Jenny was living in, and that
he was stabbed to death. I'm not sure how they got that information; maybe the cops leaked it, or maybe some enterprising
reporter dug it all out.

In any event, it doesn't matter. What happens next will depend entirely on whatever the cops uncover, and my best guess
is that it won't take long. This is the kind of situation to which
law enforcement will devote substantial resources. The pressure
on them will increase exponentially, hour after hour.

I'm the last to get up; when I go downstairs, Laurie and Jenny are sitting in the den, watching television. Ricky is in the kitchen eating cereal; I don't think he's impressed that a movie star is in the house.

When I enter the den, Jenny has the remote control in her hand and is switching channels like I do on an NFL Sunday. She gets to CNN and I am jolted by the fact that they are showing a photo of me, and not a particularly good one.

"Uh-oh," I say.

The commentator says that they have information that Jenny is being represented by Andy Carpenter, *noted criminal defense attorney from Paterson.* They go on to list a few of the clients and cases that have rendered me semi-famous, but unfortunately fail to mention that I dated Jenny in high school.

"I'd better walk the dogs before this place turns into a zoo," I say.

Jenny nods. "I'm sorry I got you into this."

"We're happy to help in any way we can," Laurie interjects, accurately.

I take Tara, Sebastian, and Hunter for our morning walk to Eastside Park. Tara and Hunter, a pug, attack the process with their normal excitement and upbeat attitude. Sebastian, a basset hound, is never pleased in situations like this, since he knows that the walk will delay breakfast. His preference would be to eat both before and after the walk, possibly also stopping for a snack along the way.

Mamie doesn't come with us; Jenny takes her into our back-yard to do her business. Fortunately, Jenny brings a plastic bag with her, because as humans we are the species that must pick up what dogs leave behind.

Of course, it's Sebastian's fault that our trip takes a long time. He walks like he's pulling a tractor trailer, which I am sure must piss off Tara and Hunter as much as it does me. Of course, the pace gives me time to think, but I don't come up with anything positive.

My instincts tell me that Jenny is in considerable trouble, and the pressure that the cops and prosecutors will feel from all the media attention is not going to help. This is not a story that is going to go away anytime soon.

I'd like to get back before the media horde assembles at my house, but Sebastian has his own agenda. "Sebastian, if you'll move your fat ass a little faster, there's an extra biscuit in it for you," I say, but if it has any effect on him it's very subtle. The problem is that he knows I am even-handed in my biscuit distribution, and I'd never give any one of the dogs more than their colleagues.

We're a block away when I see that the media mob has already started forming on the street in front of the house. I detour around to Forty-first Street so that I can come in through the back and avoid questions that I don't currently have an answer to.

We make it in without being seen, though I'm sure the media will eventually figure it out and start watching the back door. We're getting all this attention even though it hasn't yet been revealed that Jenny is staying with us; if and when that happens the neighborhood will become a complete madhouse.

Jenny comes right to the point when I get back. "They say I am a person of interest."

"I'm sure you are; the victim was in your house with you. But that does not mean you are going to be charged."

"Then what does it mean?" she asks. "Am I a suspect?"

"It means that they are going to accumulate evidence and see whether it implicates you or not."

"Do you think it will?"

"I don't have any idea. All we can do is wait and prepare for any eventuality."

"How do we do that?"

"You start by telling me about your relationship with Griffin." I'm asking this even though I'm not technically her lawyer yet, though I suspect that's where this is going.

She thinks about it for a while; it's an invasion of privacy, but nothing compared to what she will experience if she's charged. "We dated for a while."

"Seriously?"

"I thought so. Then I caught him cheating on me. I can't say it was a great surprise; his reputation preceded him. But it was still more than I was willing to put up with."

This conversation has not started well. Griffin's betrayal could be spun as a motive for murder.

"So you broke it off?"

"I did."

"Then why did you agree to make the movie with him?"

"I had signed the contract long before; I didn't have a choice. And I thought we could keep it professional."

"But it wasn't staying professional," Laurie says, her first contribution to this conversation. "That was obvious at the dinner."

"You're right, it wasn't. He wanted to pick up as if nothing had happened; I made it as clear as possible that there was no chance of that. He is . . . was . . . not the take-no-for-an-answer type. You saw that firsthand."

"Do you have any idea how he got into your house last night?" I ask. "Did he have a key?"

"He definitely did not have a key. But to be honest, I can't remember if I locked the door that night; sometimes I would forget. And there might have been a couple of windows open. I'm not a big fan of air-conditioning, and it hasn't been too hot the last few days. I know I should be more careful. But as for Ryan, I never even told him where I was staying."

"Wouldn't you have listed the address with the film production office?"

"I didn't, but maybe Linda did."

Linda Ivers is Jenny's assistant, and I make a note to ask her about the address issue.

"Who were the two guys with Griffin at Charlie's?" I ask.

"Some kind of security guys; Ryan was big on that. They were always on the set with him while we were shooting. I don't know their last names, but he called them Danny and Gurley. I guess maybe Gurley was a last name."

"I'll ask Marcus to try to locate them," Laurie says.

The phone rings and Laurie goes out of the room to answer it. She comes back moments later, holding the phone, and says, "Andy, it's for you. It's Captain Jansing."

I take the phone from her and walk out of the room to talk in privacy. "Hello?"

"I'll get right to the point," he says, getting right to the point. "We're arresting your client for the murder of Ryan Griffin."

There is no sense in me arguing the point; it's not like I'm going to be able to talk him out of it. "We want to avoid a perp walk," I say.

"I agree," he says, surprising me a bit. "If I have your word you'll bring her in, I'm good with that."

"Thank you."

We make arrangements for me to drive Jenny to the Englewood station in two hours. Jansing tells me an entrance that will be cleared, and where people will be waiting to take Jenny into custody. "So I have your word," he asks. "No white Bronco chases?"

"We'll be there."

I get off the phone and head into the den to break the news.

"We need to talk," I say.

Jenny is handling this amazingly well.

On the ride to Englewood, while admitting she is scared to death, she is calm and in apparent control. I try to explain to her what will happen when she gets there, but it's impossible for a person to be prepared for something like this.

She has not officially asked me to be her attorney and to represent her in this case; last night she was just calling me as a friend for help. So I raise the issue, and she emphatically says that she wants me to do it.

"I've followed your career some, Andy. You might not remember this, but we went on a few dates in high school."

"Really? I would have thought I'd remember something like that," I say.

"I have plenty of money to pay you, Andy. I made fifteen million dollars on my last film."

I have no interest in taking on another client; with plenty of my own money, I've been trying to retire for years. But I have less interest in letting down a friend.

We arrive at the entrance that we were told to go to, and as Griffin promised, there are no media and no outsiders. Four officers are there to greet us, and they take Jenny inside to be processed. They behave respectfully and professionally, which does not surprise me.

I remind her for the fiftieth time to talk to no one about

anything, and promise to see her tomorrow. On the way out, I stop in the office to make sure that they are giving her special treatment, keeping her away from other inmates. She needs to be protected.

They assure me that they're already doing that, and I'm not surprised. The last thing they would want is to have to publicly announce that something bad has happened to their most famous prisoner.

On the way home I call Sam Willis. Sam possesses the amazing ability to hack into pretty much any computer system on the planet, though he prefers the word *enter* instead of *hack*.

Sam is the opposite of me in a lot of ways, technology prowess being just one of them. Another significant difference between us is that he will be thrilled to hear that we have a client, while I would rather have a persistent rash.

"Sam, we have a client," I say.

"Excellent . . . talk to me."

"We're already talking, Sam."

Sam likes to speak the way he thinks a detective speaks; his goal in life is to move off the computer and work the streets. When it comes to dealing with actual physical danger, Sam is just as ill-equipped to deal with it as I am. Unfortunately, he doesn't know it. I do.

"Is this about the Griffin murder? Are we representing Jenny Nichols?"

"It is, and we are."

"Wow . . . this is great," he says.

"You took the words right out of my mouth. To start, we need to know everything we can about Ryan Griffin. Professionally and personally."

"I'm on it."

"I'm going to call a meeting of the team at ten tomorrow morning."

"Ten-four."

"No, just ten. Can you update us on what you've learned by then?"

"Roger that."

"Good. Sam, I'm about to say goodbye, so please try not to say *wilco.*"

"I hear you, Chief."

"Goodbye, Sam."

I disconnect the call before he can respond; there's at least a 60 percent chance he couldn't resist the *wilco,* but at least I'll never know.

I call Laurie and fill her in, and then she and I start making calls to the members of our team to inform them about tomorrow's meeting. She calls her K Team partners, Marcus and Corey, while I call Eddie Dowd, an attorney who works with us, and my administrative assistant, Edna.

Edna's is the toughest call to make. She dreads when we get a client because that means there is a chance she might have to do some actual work. And this is a bad time for her to be distracted by her job; she is in the middle of the second year of her engagement, and is consumed by wedding planning.

She and her fiancé have been spending most of their time traveling to potential destination wedding locations. They haven't come up with their ideal place yet, but they're making significant progress by narrowing the possibilities. They've already eliminated North Korea and Somalia.

"I knew this would happen," Edna says, stoically, when I tell her about the client. "Did you ever wake up in the morning with a terrible premonition?"

"I have, yes."

"It's just my luck that this Griffin guy went and got murdered while we're in the middle of wedding planning."

"He was an obviously inconsiderate guy, may he rest in peace," I say. "The meeting is in the office tomorrow at ten."

"Voluntary or mandatory?"

"I'm afraid it's mandatory and can't be postponed. Our client is in jail, and you know how unforgiving the legal system can be."

She sighs, loudly enough for Jenny to hear her at the jail downtown. "Okay, I'll rearrange things and be there."

"You're a trooper."

When I get home, the chaos outside the house has only increased, but this time I'm not sneaking in through the back door. I've got something to say, and after weaving my way through the crowd, I stand on our front porch and say it.

"Jenny Nichols is innocent . . . totally and completely innocent. I expect that the prosecution will come to realize that and release her with an apology, but if they don't, we will beat their ass in court.

"You can quote me on that."

There must not be anything going on in the real world. No wars, significant legislation, international incidents . . .

. . . because the Ryan Griffin murder case and Jenny's arrest are quite literally all that the news stations are covering.

Vince Sanders is especially happy since I gave him permission to publish the details of what he witnessed at Charlie's the other night. Griffin was the aggressive one and Jenny handled him calmly and without losing her cool.

I asked Vince to leave out the fact that Griffin had two security guys with him. I don't know if the cops know that yet, and I don't want to give them any help.

I gave Vince the go-ahead because the whole story will come out anyway at trial, and just in case Jenny's story changes to self-defense, it will come in handy. In any event, even though it's still somewhat incriminating, this presents it in the best possible light.

I strongly doubt it will come to a self-defense claim; Jenny is firm in her denial that she had anything to do with Griffin's death. She also did not claim self-defense when she talked to the cops; to do so now would mean that at the time she was lying and showing consciousness of guilt. In the meantime, Vince's scoop has turned him into his own mini media sensation.

Lately I've been working out of our home, for a couple of reasons. For one thing, it's a lot more comfortable than my dump of an office on Van Houten Street in downtown Paterson. For another, it's obviously far more convenient for Laurie and me, and allows us to be around more for Ricky.

Ricky's current situation is another reason we want to stay at the house as much as possible. The school year ended last week, and next week he leaves on one of those teen tours around the western United States.

I've got two problems with him going on a teen tour. For one, I am having trouble coming to grips with the fact that he's a teen; it's happening much too fast. The other problem is the tour itself; I know they're well supervised, but the idea of him out there in the world makes me anxious.

In previous years he's gone to camp for the summer, and I liked knowing where he was every second. For the tour I have his itinerary, he'll have a phone, and the tour company certainly seems to have their act together, but I'm still a nervous parent. Laurie's handling it better, which is no surprise. She's going to miss him but is happy he's going to have an enjoyable adventure.

But once Ricky leaves, and for the duration of Jenny's case, we're going to be using the office. I want to gradually demonstrate to the collective media that there is nothing to be gained from camping out at our house; I owe that much to our neighbors.

I also want to be able to come and go freely; I don't want to be followed as I go about my investigative work. There are meetings I may want to hold in secret, without the media following me and telling the whole world about it.

There are media people camped in front of my office building when Laurie and I get there. I doubt they're too impressed; I have an office above the fruit stand on the first floor operated by my landlord, Sofia Hernandez. Hopefully she'll benefit from the publicity and sell a lot of peaches and plums.

We're the first members of the team to arrive, and I watch from the window as more media people show up, obviously having been tipped off that I'm here. The other members of our team come separately, and I watch as they force their way through the crowd.

When Marcus Clark arrives, he doesn't have to do much forcing. Marcus has a presence that radiates danger, and the media Red Sea parts to let him through.

We're finally all settled in my cramped conference room. "Our client, for those of you who don't already know, is Jenny Nichols." I almost instinctively add, ". . . who I dated in high school," but I catch myself. I hope I don't blurt it out to the jury if this goes to trial.

Although Laurie, Corey, and Marcus were present at Charlie's the other night and therefore know what happened, I describe the incident for everyone else, in case they didn't read it in the paper this morning. "Later that night, Griffin was killed in the house that Jenny was staying in, which had been owned by her mother."

"The media reports him as being stabbed," Corey says, as both a statement and a question.

I nod. "In the back; it happened in the kitchen. Our client says that she arrived home from the dinner, went straight to bed, and didn't discover the body until later that night. She then called the police, and then after they arrived she called me."

Corey again: "Any idea how he got in?"

"Could have been through the front door or a window; Jenny apparently wasn't very careful about locking either. The arraignment is tomorrow, and I'll make my usual pitch to get discovery immediately. Obviously that will tell us much more."

"It's clearly a very high-profile situation, and they made a quick arrest," Corey says. "They must believe they have a powerful case."

"I'm sure they think that, but they have been wrong before. Sam, what can you tell us about Ryan Griffin?"

Sam stands and speaks, holding a notepad and glancing at it occasionally. "He was thirty-eight years old, born in Highwood, just outside of Chicago. Married twice and divorced twice, the most recent marriage lasted seven years and ended a year and a half ago. His latest ex-wife is Audrey Dodge, and she is a producing partner on a couple of his films, including the one they were making in New York. It was to be a romantic comedy called *All Together Now*."

Sam continues, "Griffin graduated from Cornell and then got an MBA from the University of Virginia. Worked in finance in New York and wound up as a partner in a hedge fund, getting very rich in the process.

"According to articles, Griffin always had a dream of making it in Hollywood as an actor; he was active in theater in college. But when he finally went out there, it was primarily as a producer. He was that rare producer who financed his own films, maybe with his own money or maybe with help from outside investors. Or a combination of both.

"He gave roles to himself in some of them, and based on critical reaction, he had some talent. The films have been mixed in terms of box-office sales, but he was churning them out, and had many more in development."

He holds up a folder and says, "There's more detail in here, but those are the basics, for now. I didn't get a chance to make copies."

"Edna," I say.

"What?"

"Can you make copies for everyone?"

"Now?"

"Now would be a good time, yes."

Dedicated employee that she is, Edna takes the folder and goes off to the outer office, where the copy machine is.

"Okay, that's it for now," I say. "Once again, we'll know much more when we get discovery, and I'll be heading down to the jail to talk to our client. I'll keep everyone up to date and will give out investigation assignments when I am better informed."

I adjourn the meeting, but I have an uneasy feeling because of something Corey said. The police would not have made such a quick arrest in a case with this much public attention if they didn't believe they had a slam dunk.

I'm not looking forward to finding out why they think so.

Until this morning, I never realized that the Bergen County Courthouse was the center of the universe.

I don't come here often because most of my cases are in Passaic County, which is where Paterson is located. But while this is an impressive building on Main Street in Hackensack, it's never seemed anything out of the ordinary.

That was true until today.

Today it is an absolute circus.

It takes me twenty minutes to walk the five hundred feet from the parking lot to the courthouse entrance. I have to disregard what seems like thousands of questions, and while I don't keep a detailed record of them, it seems like the one most frequently asked is, *How will she plead?*

If this is the coverage for the arraignment, I cannot imagine what a trial would be like. Nothing of real consequence is going to happen today. Jenny will enter a plea of *not guilty,* but even that has no great significance. If we were trying to negotiate a plea for her, which we are not, she would still register as not guilty until the time that the plea deal was set in stone.

Eddie Dowd is already at the defense table when I arrive. I had asked him to get the judge to allow Jenny to wear her normal clothing to all court sessions, and he tells me that the request was granted.

The lead prosecutor on the case is James Shaffer. We've met

a few times, but I don't know him well. We've never gone up against each other on a case, again because I rarely work in Bergen County.

But Shaffer is considered the star of the prosecutor's office, which explains why he has been given this case. Everything all of us do will be under a microscope, so the county will want to make sure it puts its best foot forward. Bergen County has decided that their best foot is Shaffer.

Jenny has decided that her best foot is Carpenter.

May the best foot win.

Shaffer comes over to say hello, and we shake hands. "There seems to be some interest in this one," he says, smiling.

"No more than usual," I say. "I attract this kind of attention wherever I go."

Jenny is brought in and she takes her seat between Eddie and me. She looks fine, but I can see the strain and fear in her eyes. I don't know if anyone else can see it, but I know her very well.

I dated her in high school.

I explain to her what will happen today, which isn't much. Some motions have been filed and will be argued, but nothing terribly significant. Jenny will plead and a trial date will be set, and that will be that.

"Will I get bail?" she asks.

"We'll certainly give it our best shot, but it could go either way."

"Please push for it. It's horrible here."

"Have you been mistreated in any way?"

"No, actually everyone has been very nice and respectful. But not being able to go anywhere, to be imprisoned . . . it's just the worst thing I have ever experienced."

"I understand."

I go on to tell her not to show any emotion, to just take

things in stride without reacting. "Every eye in the room will be on you; it's important that you don't give them anything to talk about and analyze." It's never easy for any person on trial in a case of this kind, but Jenny is an actress, so I hope and expect she can pull it off.

"I understand," she says.

I tell her that when she says *not guilty,* she should do so with conviction, but not be overly dramatic.

"You should have been a director," she says, and then as the judge is coming in, she asks, "How's Mamie?"

"Adorable. And I think she and Hunter have a thing going."

Judge Margaret Slater enters, looking very serious and businesslike. I think they teach a course in judge school on looking stern, and if so, Judge Slater aced it. The look on her face says that she doesn't care how famous this case and defendant are, her court will not be a circus.

I've never met Judge Slater, so I've not yet given her a reason to dislike me. Hopefully that means I'm starting with a clean slate, but if she has any judge friends in Passaic County, I'm in trouble. Let's just say that Passaic County judges would not offer a ringing endorsement of my courtroom manner.

The clerk reads the charges against Jenny, by far the most significant being first-degree murder. There is a murmur coming from the gallery when this is said, but it stops quickly with just a stare from Judge Slater. Judge Slater can stare with the best of them.

She has only a few perfunctory motions to deal with. I haven't asked for a change of venue because the publicity would be great in every city in America, and at least here Jenny has the advantage of being the hometown girl.

Judge Slater clearly believes in moving things along quickly, and after a few housekeeping matters, she asks Jenny to stand

and tell the court how she pleads. Jenny's *not guilty* is perfect, defiant but respectful, firm but not over the top.

The judge asks if we have anything to bring up before she sets a trial date, and I get to my feet. "Two things, Your Honor. Mr. Shaffer has seen fit to charge Ms. Nichols with a serious crime, but hasn't gotten around to telling her why he is making the accusation. We have not yet received a single page of discovery."

"Mr. Shaffer," the judge asks, turning to him.

"It is being processed even as we speak, Your Honor."

"Respectfully, that is not good enough, Your Honor," I say, registering my fake outrage. "The defense is in the dark as to the prosecution's evidence and theories. It did not prevent Ms. Nichols from entering her not-guilty plea, because she already knows that she is not guilty. But the lack of discovery most certainly does impact our ability to demonstrate that innocence to the court."

"The defense will have the relevant information today, Your Honor," Shaffer says, confidently.

"Good. See that they do. Anything else?"

"Yes," I say. "We request that bail be granted and Ms. Nichols be released immediately."

Shaffer shakes his head. "The prosecution is very much opposed to that, Your Honor, both due to the nature of the crime and the fact that Ms. Nichols's considerable resources make her a flight risk."

"Mr. Carpenter?"

"First of all, while the crime was horrible, the good news is that Ms. Nichols did not commit it," I say. "She is innocent until proven guilty, and she will not be proven guilty.

"She does in fact have considerable resources as a result of her talent and hard work. But her career accomplishments should not result in her being incarcerated, while a less successful person would not be. In any event, we would not object to bail being set at a high level. High, but reasonable."

"And the risk of flight?" Judge Slater asks.

I frown to demonstrate my fake disdain. "Your Honor, while I am sure a lot of words will be spoken in this courtroom before this matter is resolved, Mr. Shaffer's portrayal of Ms. Nichols as a flight risk is the leader in the clubhouse for most ridiculous.

"Ms. Nichols's face is on almost every magazine in America, and the coverage of this case is over the top. Is she going to hide somewhere, unrecognized? She is known all over the world, but we would not object to her passport being held by the court; Ms. Nichols is going to stay right here and prove her innocence."

Judge Slater grants bail at $2.5 million, to be put up in full, and Jenny will be electronically monitored. She and I consult briefly, and we agree that she will stay at our house. I have no doubt that Laurie will be fine with it.

I ask that Shaffer and I approach the bench, and when we do so I get the judge to go along with Jenny serving her house arrest at the Carpenter residence. She also goes along with a gag order on that information, so that Shaffer cannot share it with the media.

Judge Slater also takes the opportunity to caution us against fanning the media flames. "I'm not issuing a public-statement gag order at this point, but I will if I have to. But I still caution each of you very strongly not to attempt to manipulate the media coverage. It will not be tolerated. Is that understood?"

We both say that it is well understood, and that's the end of this mini conference. When I get back to the table, I tell Jenny the bail arrangement.

"Thank you, Andy. You were great," she says.

I shrug modestly. "Just another day at the office."

Laurie and Corey Douglas have accomplished an amazing feat.

Both ex-cops, they've utilized their connections with the department to get them to set up a security zone in front of our house, keeping the media a reasonable distance away. We will have unimpeded access, though we'll still be verbally bombarded.

When we get home, I park in the attached garage so that Jenny can sneak in without being seen, even by the binocular-carrying press. I don't follow along; instead I walk down the street to address the crowd.

"You can obviously stay here as long as you want, but you'll be wasting your time," I say. "Miss Nichols is staying at another location," I lie, "and I won't be commenting any more either."

I don't expect my words to have any immediate effect, but maybe over time they'll come to believe that I was telling the truth and leave. Then maybe my neighbors will even stop hating me.

When I get inside, Jenny is watching Mamie attempt to play with Sebastian. Sebastian is just lying down on his side, his favorite position, while Mamie runs around him, trying to get him to play. She doesn't know it yet, but she has more chance of getting a response from a clothes hamper.

Sebastian couldn't care less about whatever Mamie might be doing; he's just wondering what time dinner is. Jenny is wearing the ankle monitoring bracelet, and seeing it reminds me I need to tell her that in the future she should wear pants over it so that Sebastian isn't tempted to take a bite out of it.

Tara stands off to the side, watching the scene and Mamie with some puzzlement, as if wondering what that crazy little white thing is.

Laurie and Ricky are in Ricky's room as they pack suitcases. He's not leaving for a week, but Laurie has always been an early packer. I'm sure he won't wear half the clothes she sends with him, but he's learned to humor her in these situations.

I approach Jenny and ask, "So are you ready to talk? Or do you want some time to relax?"

"Let's talk," Jenny says. "I want to be as helpful as possible."

"Okay, good. Tell me all about Ryan Griffin."

"The personal side or the professional side?"

"Is there a difference?" I ask.

"Probably not. His key attribute in both areas was how charismatic he was. Incredibly charming; what you saw the other night at dinner was not who he was. He hasn't been himself for a while."

"Why not?"

"I'm not really sure. There was some drug involvement . . . I know that. It was increasing, and it's another one of the things that broke us up. He promised to stop but I don't believe he did.

"But he was also under some kind of external pressure that he never shared with me. Whatever the problem was, he was not handling it well." Then, "But the Ryan Griffin I knew, or thought I knew, could be thoughtful and considerate."

"Is that why you agreed to do the film? Or was it just the contract?"

"It was both, and I also really liked the script. I had signed the contract before I broke off our personal relationship.

"Once rehearsal started, I could see that it was not going to work out. He was erratic and disrespectful, borderline abusive both to me and others. It was uncharacteristic, but I wasn't going to put up with it. I had told him I was leaving the day before he died; that I couldn't accept the atmosphere on the set."

"How did he react to that?"

She smiles sadly. "Not well. Not well at all."

"Couldn't the director control him?"

"If he could, he chose not to. Keep in mind that Ryan was functioning in two roles, both producer and actor. He chose and hired the director and could have fired him if he had wanted to."

"And it was all his own money?" I ask.

"Yes, although I'm sure he had investors. Money was not a problem for Ryan, which is the key in Hollywood."

"What do you mean?"

"There are two categories—the ones who have money and the ones who need it. And when I say need it, I'm not talking about for food or shelter. I'm talking about the ability to make a movie. The studios have the money; individual actors and producers do not. So the studios, and now the streaming services, have the upper hand, the power to say yes or no to a project."

She continues, "Ryan was the exception; he could make whatever movies he wanted, within reason. He didn't need anyone else to green-light them."

"When he was at the dinner the other night and wanted you to leave with him, was he acting as your ex-boyfriend or the producer of the movie?"

She thinks about the question for a short while. "I don't know; and I don't think he knew. The two were tied together.

This is going to be my last time at Charlie's for a while.

Once I get deeply into trial preparation, normal living becomes impossible. For me, watching sports, drinking beer, eating burgers and fries, and insulting my friends pass for normal living.

Vince Sanders is at our regular table along with Pete Stanton, a captain in the Paterson PD, homicide division. Lately, I haven't been coming here that often, at least compared to them. They have a perfect attendance record.

But they have kept my chair empty and unused, which is less a tribute to me than an acknowledgment of the fact that they put all their food and beer on my tab.

"Well, if it isn't Mr. Hollywood," Pete says when I arrive.

"Leave him alone," Vince says. "He gave me a story. That was quite a dinner party."

"How come you didn't invite me?" Pete asks.

"Invite you?" I ask. "Have you looked in a mirror? Have you ever heard yourself talk? Jenny is a friend; I wouldn't subject her to that."

"But you invite Vince?"

"That's actually something for you to think about." I point to Vince and say, "I obviously thought that this slovenly moron was less embarrassing than you. That might give you incentive to make some personal changes."

"Yeah," Vince says. "You tell him, Andy."

"How about if the first change is I rearrange your face," Pete asks.

"Not what I had in mind," I say.

"So you have any more scoops for me?" Vince asks.

"Yeah. Jenny is innocent and we're going to prove it."

Pete laughs. "Yeah, her ex-boyfriend who cheated on her gets stabbed in the back in her kitchen with no one else home. A real whodunit."

I have no answer to that, so as I turn toward one of the many televisions I say, "The talking phase of this meeting is over. I'm going to watch the Mets."

I just watch a couple of innings and then leave to work on the case. When I get home I'm surprised to see that Jenny has a visitor. It's Linda Ivers, Jenny's personal assistant on the film they were shooting in New York, as well as previous ones.

Jenny has described her as incredibly competent and helpful, eager to tackle any job she is given.

She is the anti-Edna.

"Linda came over to see if I needed anything," Jenny says. "I told her that I'm being well taken care of."

I tell Linda that I'm glad she's here, because I want to ask her some questions. She seems a bit worried about it. "What about? I don't know anything."

"Just background," I say.

"Let's go into the den," I say to Linda, and she follows me in there. I think Jenny wants to come along, but she waits for an invite that is not forthcoming. I want Linda to tell me the truth, not what she thinks Jenny wants to hear.

Once we're settled in the den, I ask how long Linda has known Jenny. "About three years," she says. "I've been her assistant on four films, and between films as well. I love her; she's the absolute best."

"She's been good to you?"

"Very. Some stars, not nearly as big as Jenny, have an ego that causes them to not be nice to people. Jenny's not like that; you hang out with her, you would never know she's Jenny Nichols, movie star. She's just like anybody else." She smiles. "Except for the paparazzi."

"So you've seen her with Ryan Griffin?"

She nods. "A lot. I hope I'm not talking out of turn, but I never understood it."

"What do you mean?"

"Jenny could have had anyone, but for a while, at least, she chose him. And he wasn't always nice to her; sometimes he could be verbally abusive. And he cheated on her."

"You know that for a fact?"

She nods. "I know another woman he was with. And I've heard the stories; everybody's heard the stories. He didn't just cheat on Jenny; he cheated on Audrey and everyone else he was ever with."

I can already tell that I would have to think long and hard before putting Linda Ivers on the stand. On the one hand, she would make a good character witness for Jenny; she obviously likes her and the jury would like to hear that Jenny is a good, unassuming person, without an outsized ego.

On the other, more important hand, her talk of Ryan verbally abusing Jenny and cheating on her would feed right into the prosecution's theory of motive, that Jenny was a woman wronged.

It will be a tough call whether to put her on or not, but she might be reading my mind, because she asks, "Can I testify for Jenny?"

"What about?"

"I can tell everyone what a great and generous person she is, how she doesn't have a mean bone in her body, and could never hurt anyone. Jenny has given me everything; I would do anything to help her."

"Maybe," I say, mostly to end the conversation. "I might want to call you to testify."

She smiles. "I hope so."

I talk to her for a while more, in the hope that she might have some significant observations of Ryan from her time around him. She has no firsthand knowledge of his drug use, though of course she has heard the rumors. And of course she has no idea where his money comes from.

"By the way, did you list the address of the house where Jenny was staying with the production company?"

She shakes her head vigorously. "No chance. I put down the hotel where I was staying. If they wanted to see Jenny, they had to go through me."

"Okay, thanks," I say. "Any moral support you can give Jenny I'm sure would be appreciated."

"I wish I could be more help," she says. "Jenny could not have done . . . what they are saying. It's just not possible."

"If you don't testify, I'll try and get you on the jury."

The discovery documents have arrived, which unfortunately means I have to read them.

Eddie Dowd has come over this morning to share in the agony, and we start to plow through everything. It doesn't take much plowing; there's not that much here. But what there is can be described as decidedly unpleasant.

A good part of it is what is not technically here, which is the prosecution's theory of the case. But everything we read points directly to that theory in a way that very few jurors could miss. To prevail, I would have to get a jury of twelve total morons, and in most cases I can't count on more than five or six.

To start, there is the fact that a dead body, with blood everywhere, was lying on the floor of Jenny's kitchen. There is no evidence, and no claim by Jenny, that anyone else was in the house. There is also blood in the sink, and some on Jenny's clothing.

Jenny's words that night are devastating, at least in the eyes of the prosecution. She answered the questions the police asked her, before I had a chance to tell her otherwise. They recorded the conversation and did so properly, alerting her to the fact that she was being recorded.

The audio has her saying that she was in the house for almost three hours without noticing the body, but that she has no idea how Griffin got in the house in the first place.

She told the cops that he did not have a key, yet there was no evidence that any entry point, window or door, was tampered with. There are also no fingerprints on those potential entrances that might indicate otherwise. The only prints in the house were those of Jenny and Griffin, and all of his were in the kitchen.

Jenny has since told me that there have been times she forgot to lock the door, and that she might have left windows open. She had not mentioned that to the cops. I believe her, but the jury will find it somewhat less than credible.

The kitchen has yielded other problems for the defense. On the table were two coffee cups, each with a small amount of coffee left in them. If Jenny was alone, who was drinking from the other cup?

There were also two cake plates with crumbs still on them, and the remainder of the cake itself on a large plate in the center. The cake had obviously been cut to yield the pieces, which leads to the worst fact of all.

The knife that cut the cake is the one that was planted in Griffin's back and wound up on the floor next to him; forensics confirms that fact.

It has been a while since I read something this depressing.

"This is an uphill climb," Eddie says when we're finished. "And her words lock her in."

"I know." What Eddie means is that Jenny has already told her story, whether or not it makes sense. It would be hard at this point to claim that she killed Griffin in self-defense after saying that she did not. The fact that she waited hours to report it doesn't work in favor of self-defense either. If she were to claim it now, it would mean that she lied to the cops, which by itself shows consciousness of guilt.

Not that it matters much; under any circumstances it would be difficult to convince a jury that she feared for her life from an assailant, but wound up stabbing him in the back.

Our job is to figure out and demonstrate how Griffin happened to be there without Jenny knowing it, how a killer appeared on the scene as well, and how it is that Jenny's cake knife was the murder weapon.

I definitely need to talk to Jenny about all of this, though I suspect she will just be bewildered by it all. That won't tell me much about whether or not she is actually guilty. If she's telling the truth, which is what I believe to be the case, then she would be unable to explain any of it, because she genuinely has no idea.

Jenny's been watching the television coverage almost non-stop. I don't know if that is a positive for her mental state or not, but I certainly don't want to intervene. She has to do what she needs to do. But I interrupt her viewing to talk to her about the discovery.

"The prosecution has shown us their evidence. I'm sure they are still investigating, but this is where they are right now."

She looks wary. "I've got a feeling I'm not going to like this."

"You're not," I say. I describe for her the scene in the kitchen, and the coffee setting for two on the table. She was obviously in the kitchen that night; she discovered the body. But in the shock of seeing Griffin and all the blood, she very well might not have noticed the details.

She shakes her head emphatically. "It's not true," she says. "I had coffee before I left, but there was no other setting. I was alone."

I show her a photo that the police took of the table, which clearly contradicts her recollection.

"Andy, I am telling you, there was no second cup, and that cake was back in the refrigerator."

"The knife that cut the cake was the one that killed Griffin."

She physically recoils from that. "My God," she says, in obvious horror. I'm not sure why she has that reaction; the knife had to come from somewhere, and I don't know why she should have any personal connection to a cake knife.

"Do you have any insights at all into what might be going on here?" I ask.

"You can't imagine how much I wish I did, but I don't. Somebody wanted to make it look like I killed Ryan, but I just have no idea why."

I nod with an obvious lack of enthusiasm, and she asks, "Andy, you don't think I did this, do you?"

When I don't quickly answer, she says, "Andy, there is simply no way I could plunge a knife into a human being. Not anyone, not for any reason. I don't understand how anyone could do that."

The truth is that I do believe her; I just can't help looking at it through a juror's eyes, and from that vantage point, I don't like what I see.

I can't just tell a jury to trust me on this one.

Going to a murder scene is like going to Madison Square Garden the morning after a typical Knicks game.

You know that something really depressing and ugly happened there the night before, but at the moment it's quiet and sterile. Instead of beer cups and popcorn kernels on the ground, there is blood spatter and chalk outlines.

Actually, a more serious murder scene/sports analogy might be to compare it to going to a football game. You can watch a game on television and see every play, including countless replays. But when you go to a game in person, you see the big picture. You can watch the whole field and not just follow the ball, as they mostly do on television.

A murder scene is similar, in that you can learn all the facts from the discovery. The police photograph the scene exhaustively, and technically everything is covered. But it is still not the same as going there, because by being on the scene, one gets to see the big picture.

Of course, I'm not a detective, so examining murder scenes is not my specialty. Being obnoxious in court is my specialty. So I always bring Laurie along with me; she has a much better understanding of what we're looking at.

We've gone together to many of these; it's become like a couples thing that we share. It's not really romantic; the blood stains and gore really put a damper on that. So we try to remain professional when we're on-site; we don't even call each other pet names.

This outing is different from the norm in that I've been to this scene before. I was here at Jenny's house the night Griffin died, but I did not actually go inside. She was in the police car and I was intent on getting her out of there before she could do any more talking.

I wish I had gotten here sooner.

There is still a police presence on the scene. Tape is up and there is a cop guarding the front door. I'm not sure how the tape helps him do so; even I could walk through it. Or under it. But someone obviously spent the money to order the tape, so they must feel obligated to use it.

Laurie knows the cop from her time on the force; his name is Billy Wilhelm, so he smiles as they wave at each other. "We used to call him Billy Willy," she says.

"You cops are incredibly clever."

Before we approach the front door, we stop to take in the surroundings. The house is set far off the street, and it's highly unlikely that anyone walking by at night could have seen anything going on near the house. Of course, the nearest houses are so far away that it would be a surprise if anyone was walking in the area in the first place.

"How did Griffin get here?" Laurie asks. "Was his car here?"

"Not when the police came."

She nods. "Good. The presence of his car would have made Jenny's claim that she didn't know anyone was here even harder to believe."

"The discovery did not speak to how he got here, so they probably don't know yet. He could have been dropped off by the two security goons who were with him at Charlie's."

"So they drop him off and he has no key, but somehow he gets in the house," Laurie says.

"Jenny said that she sometimes forgot to lock the door and left windows open."

Laurie frowns. "Not smart."

"I know," I say. "And now she does also. Let's go check it out."

We walk to the front door and Billy Willy lets us in after exchanging *how are you*s with Laurie. He had known we were coming, since we had gotten the approval from Shaffer's office. Once inside, we walk along the perimeter. The house is very large; I count twenty-two first-floor windows.

There is fingerprint powder on all of them; if Griffin or his killer entered through one of them, they didn't leave prints. The same thing is true of the back door, which leads out to a patio and swimming pool.

But they could have just walked in through the front door, if Jenny in fact hadn't locked it. Or if she had, they could have come through a window and wiped their prints; they wouldn't have to be master criminals to know enough to do that.

"This is a lot nicer than the house Jenny grew up in in Paterson," I say. Then, "Time to check out the kitchen."

It's a big house, so we wander about a bit before we find the kitchen. Once we do, Laurie says, "It makes sense that if Jenny didn't come in here when she got home, then she would not have known about the body. It's far from the front door and the staircase leading up to the bedroom."

"Chalk up one for our side," I say.

The blood stains leave no doubt where Griffin's body was. He bled a lot, which can happen when someone has a knife plunged into them.

"He was stabbed in the back, which means he was facing

those cabinets. Clearly not trying to run out of the house or escape," Laurie says.

"Right."

"His head was wedged back against the table. If he was moving or running away, his body would have fallen forward."

Laurie is looking at the table. The cups and plates are gone, obviously taken as evidence. It's all been memorialized in photographs, which both Laurie and I have seen. It's a fairly long table and slightly narrow, which I assume was done to fit the shape of the kitchen.

"The cups were there and there," she says, pointing to the opposite ends. "Seems strange that if two people were having coffee, they would sit so far apart like that." She points again. "They could have sat there and there, still without being too close."

"It had to have been staged," I say. "But we're a long way from proving it."

I look over and see that the machine to make the coffee is a Keurig, which makes coffee a cup at a time. There is a used pod still in the machine. "Go get your friend Billy."

Laurie doesn't ask why; she knows that it will be clear soon enough. She leaves and a short while later comes back with Billy.

"Officer, I'm going to open that trash door," I say. "We just need you to witness it and see what's in there. Laurie, can you record this?"

"Why?" he asks.

"Just want it clear that we're not tampering with anything."

"Okay."

I open the door and pull out the trash bin; there's a plastic garbage bag lining it, but the bag is completely empty. "Empty, right?"

He looks in and says, "Empty."

"Any sign that anything was in here? Any stains? Maybe coffee stains, or wet spots?"

He looks into the bin more carefully and says, "No. The bag seems refreshed and so far unused."

"So this pod in the machine is the only one here?"

He nods. "Right. That's all I see."

"Thank you, Officer. That's all we needed." I motion to Laurie that she can stop filming.

Billy goes back to his post, and Laurie asks, "What was that about?"

"I don't remember anything about the trash contents in the discovery, though I have to recheck it. My guess is that it was empty, like it is now, so there was nothing for them to report."

"And?"

"And there was no second Keurig pod; just the one in the machine. Two people would have meant two pods."

"Not bad," she says.

"Aw, shucks."

'm not looking forward to my phone call with Robby Divine.

Robby is the wealthiest man I know . . . one of the wealthiest that anyone knows. Money is the way he keeps score; it's a game to him that he always wins.

We met at a charity dinner one night and hit it off, and he has been very helpful to me when I've called on him ever since. I am also quite well off, due to an inheritance and some lucrative cases, but compared to Robby I am a street urchin begging for porridge.

The reason I am dreading the call is that Robby's beloved Chicago Cubs are in the middle of a six-game losing streak, which has come well into an overall losing season. Robby is a Cubs fanatic; if there was a stronger word than *fanatic* I would use it.

"How are you?" I ask, knowing what the answer will be.

"How am I? Do you not read the papers? Are you even aware there is a sports section?"

"I am vaguely aware, and I'm sorry about the Cubs. Maybe they will turn it around," I say, knowing that they won't.

Robby calls me on it. "They will not turn it around. They are pointed in one direction, and it ain't up."

"I have a possible solution. Why don't you buy the team?" I ask.

"And then who would I blame if we lost?"

"Good point."

"Let me guess," he says. "You're calling for a favor or information."

"What tipped you off?"

"Next question."

"I need to see Martin Runyon for a case I'm working on, but he'll duck me. I was hoping you could fix that."

"What am I, your appointments secretary?"

"Not at all, but you'd be a damn good one."

"Is this about the Griffin murder?"

Griffin was Runyon's partner atop a hedge fund before Griffin went off to Hollywood. "It is," I say.

"Griffin was an asshole."

"You're speaking ill of the dead."

"I am aware of that, but dying does not offer one conversational immunity. The cemeteries are filled with dead assholes."

"What about Martin Runyon?" I ask. "What kind of guy is he?"

"Decent guy. Smart, conservative, boring, doesn't take risks."

"So can you get him to see me?"

"Obviously. Call him in the morning."

Click.

At this stage, my approach will be to find out whatever I can about the victim. If Jenny did not kill him, and I strongly believe she did not, then someone else did. The more I learn about Griffin, the better chance I'll have to find out who would have wanted him dead.

I've already started the process of moving our base of operations into my office downtown. Jenny will always be around the house; she is legally unable to leave even if she wanted to. I can't have her overhearing our discussions about her case. There is a definite danger of, at the least, her misunderstanding what we are saying, and at worst, her trying to influence the investigation.

Even more important, we need to be able to talk freely, and Jenny's presence could inhibit that. It's nothing against her; it would be true of any client. Using the office will be an inconvenience, but not as bad as if Ricky were going to be home.

He's leaving tomorrow for the teen tour. I have this irrational fear that he's leaving a little kid, but in eight weeks is going to come back twenty-two years old, with a full beard, wanting his own apartment.

I'm not handling this well at all.

Ricky seems a little nervous this morning, and I don't blame him.

It's a big deal for a kid to go on his first trip alone, especially one that is going to last eight weeks. I'm not sure I would have had the guts to do it when I was his age. I'm not sure I'd have the guts to do it now.

He has to be at Newark Airport at eight o'clock to meet the group, so I get up really early and take the dogs for a walk. Mamie doesn't come with us; she prefers to do her business in the backyard. I expect Sebastian to complain and say, *How come she doesn't have to go,* but so far he's been pretty stoic about it.

The airport is about forty minutes from our house at this hour, and we are able to navigate the maze that is Newark Airport and still arrive a half hour before the appointed time. Ricky has been uncharacteristically quiet in the car; I'm half hoping that he'll tell me that we should turn around and go home, that he simply cannot bear to leave his father, but he doesn't.

We get inside the airport, and Ricky's nervousness seems to evaporate completely. He sees his best friend Will Rubenstein, who is going on the trip with him, as well as other friends he knows.

Just based on their interactions, it's obvious that he's going to have a great time, and at one point he looks back at us as if to say, *You're still here?* The people who work for Rein Teen Tours are here in force, and really seem like they are in charge and know what they're doing.

Ricky finally comes over and hugs us goodbye, and we tell him that we love him. Then we watch him go off with the leaders of the group and the rest of the kids.

This father thing is not easy.

On the way home I try to imagine how I would have been feeling in Ricky's situation. One year I had the option of going to overnight camp, but didn't go because it meant that I wouldn't be home to play little league baseball. Looking back, I think there might have been more to it than that; I might have been nervous about going away for so long.

But Ricky has been to camp the last two summers and did not seem to have any problem. He is able to self-confidently embrace the adventure, and enjoy himself. I hope he approaches this with the same attitude . . . all signs are that he will.

Laurie interrupts my obsessing with a question. "Jenny asked if she could work with me on the vegetable garden. Would that be allowed by the court?"

"I'm sure it would be fine," I say. "She'll still be on our property, so it won't set the electronic alarm off."

"Good. She seemed really anxious. Being cooped up is going to get to her; I can tell. And I can't say I blame her."

"And you think gardening will help?"

"I do, but she certainly does. She says she has a large vegetable garden in California."

When we get home, Laurie tells Jenny the great news and they head out to the backyard to do whatever it is to be done out there.

I have to admit that I don't understand the whole gardening thing, especially growing vegetables. Flowers I sort of get; they're pretty and colorful and some people, not me, like to look at them. I see them as something that every day gets closer to a wilting, miserable death.

I'm an upbeat kind of guy.

Laurie has been growing vegetables over the course of weeks, if not months, that she could buy at the supermarket in ten minutes. I could understand it for someone who cannot afford to do that; then growing their own food makes sense. But thankfully that is not us.

So I once asked Laurie what she gets out of it, and she rattled off a whole list of stuff. The conversation didn't go terribly well.

Her first reason was that it gave her time to think. "About vegetables?" I asked.

"No. About whatever is on my mind."

"You have to sit in dirt to do that?"

"That actually helps, Andy. The soil makes me feel better."

"Isn't dirt the reason that they invented soap? There's an entire section in the pharmacy of products whose only purpose is to get dirt off of people."

"There are studies that say soil on the hands releases serotonin that travels to the brain," she says. "It's a happy, peaceful chemical."

"Can't you just buy a bottle of the stuff?" I ask. "You could drink it and be happy and clean. And you wouldn't have to deal with mosquitoes and the hot sun."

She ignored that and spoke about the health benefits of eating homegrown food. I pointed out that there's already a stand in the produce section of the supermarket that sells locally grown stuff, though the truth is that I think it might be a scam, since Paterson is basically all cement.

I could see she was getting frustrated and annoyed; I have a lot of experience with people feeling that way during conversations with me. She took one more shot at it. "It gives me a feeling of satisfaction, Andy."

"I can understand that," I said. "I feel that way when I put my credit card in that little machine at the supermarket. It takes a few seconds, and I always have this image of some executives sitting around a table trying to decide if they should give me the credit. And then it says *approved,* and it makes me feel good, and validated, and happy, even though I'm not sitting in dirt."

I forget what Laurie said in response to that, but I think it was something like, *You're an asshole, Andy.*

So now it turns out that Jenny also likes to play in dirt, and if the judge is okay with that, then it's fine with me. And maybe we can use it in an insanity defense.

Sure enough, Martin Runyon is suddenly willing to meet with me, just as Robby Divine promised.

His assistant called me yesterday afternoon to tell me that he'd be available in his office at Causeway Capital on Forty-eighth and Park in Manhattan.

I left two hours early and made it here in forty-five minutes. If I had left forty-five minutes early, it would have taken me two hours. The New York/New Jersey traffic gods have designed things that way.

In my experience with companies like this, the offices are designed to give one of two impressions. Sometimes they are sleek and modern, chrome and glass everywhere, in order to make viewers think that they are high-tech and cutting edge.

Other times they are classy and stately, polished wood and mahogany abounding, to give the confident feeling of old money, which is every bit as good as new money, and less likely to disappear.

Causeway Capital has gone the elegant look, no doubt designed to make the investor feel that if the company has held on to their money this long, they will be less likely to screw up in the future. In the process of achieving this feeling, Causeway must spend more money on wood furnisher polish than I do on office rent.

Martin Runyon, when I'm brought back to his office, fits the surroundings perfectly. His suit is so perfectly tailored that he seems to have been poured into it. It probably cost so much that he should keep it in a safe-deposit box, yet I have a feeling that he has a closet full of them.

His gray hair is perfectly coiffed, and his fingernails, should I be so inclined to look at them, are probably manicured. I've never been to his house, but I would bet that it is impossible to take five steps without walking into a mirror.

It must be so exhausting for him to get ready for work each day that I feel sorry for him, even though Forbes says he is worth $900 million. He'd be worth a lot more if he wore sweatpants and cut his own hair.

Once we've dispensed with the *hello*s, he says, "So you used Robby Divine to get to me."

"I'm ruthless that way," I say.

"Robby says you are worth talking to."

"I can feel myself blushing."

Runyon has already looked at his watch three times since we started talking. Unless he's boiling a three-minute egg under his desk, he's showing me how little time he has for me. It's getting on my nerves.

"What is it with him and the Cubs?" he asks. "I told him he should buy the damn team. He sure as hell could afford it."

"I told him the same thing, but if he bought them and then still lost to the Cardinals, he would not be able to handle it. Which brings us to Ryan Griffin," I say, trying to move this along.

"It does?"

"Sorry, segues are not my specialty. Griffin was your partner?"

Runyon nods, then checks his watch again. "We started the firm together."

"How did you come to do that?"

"We worked together at another fund. Ryan was about ten years younger than me; I was sort of a mentor to him. We were doing great, but the firm wasn't, and they screwed us on our bonuses. We decided that we wanted to be the ones to decide on our own bonuses, so we left and started this place."

"And it's worked out well."

He shrugs in an unsuccessful reach for modesty, and checks his watch. "Every day is a new day."

"Have you got a pen?" I ask. "I want to write that down. *Every day is a new day*. It's a great line to use at cocktail parties, or if I find myself at the Algonquin Round Table."

"You're wearing out your welcome," he says.

"I hate when that happens. Why did Griffin leave the firm?"

"I'm not sure I know the full answer to that. He said he was bored, and I suspect that was true, but that couldn't have been all of it. He didn't punch a clock here; he could have lived a full, satisfying life outside of work."

"So what's your best guess?" I ask.

"We were very different people. I'm very private; I live a quiet life. Ryan spent his time searching for spotlights to bask in. Add to that the fact that he always wanted to be an actor, and Hollywood made perfect sense for him. That was especially true after Ryan became wealthy. There has never been a red carpet that Ryan didn't want to walk on."

"Have you had any involvement in the entertainment business?"

"I've done some investing, as has our company."

"How did you do?"

"I've broken even, which for an outsider in Hollywood is a victory. The company has done even better than that; we are more risk averse."

"You're not enamored of the movie business?"

"I've found that executives out there are either business oriented or creative, never both. They therefore have a tendency to clash with the type that they are not. But Ryan was different. He had the money, the business acumen, and maybe the talent to have it all out there."

He checks his watch yet again, and I tell him it's forty-five seconds later than the last time he looked. A less patient person, like maybe Willie Miller, would have already strangled him with the watch.

"So it would have been his own money that he was using to finance these pictures?" I ask. I already know that's the case; I want to see if Runyon will be forthcoming, in addition to being annoying.

"I don't know that one way or the other."

"Could the same people who invest money in your firm have been his investors?"

He shrugs. "Anything's possible."

"Who might those people be?"

"We do not disclose the names of the people or firms that trust us with their money. As a private company, we don't have to."

"Any idea who might have wanted him dead?" I ask. It's a question I always ask on every case, and the next time I get a meaningful and helpful response will be the first.

"Well, he certainly had his share of romantic relationships that did not end with women singing his praises. But beyond that, no. You have to understand that it was impossible to dislike Ryan."

"Someone did," I point out.

He nods. "Clearly. So let me put that another way; it was impossible not to be drawn to him on some level. He was amazingly charismatic."

Jenny had described him the same way. "A good thing to be in your business," I say.

He nods. "No question. I've seen him in meetings with people who I thought there was no chance would ever invest, and after one dinner they had their checkbook out. If you had met him you'd know what I mean."

I don't bother pointing out that I did meet him, at Charlie's, and I was able to resist his personal magnetism.

"Someone put a knife in his back," I say, pointing out the obvious. Again.

He nods. "Horrible but true. I have no idea who did that, whether it was your client or someone else, but if it was some-how related to his business life, I very much doubt it was this business, or even this city. It would have had to be out in La La Land."

Technically, in cases like this the defense is supposed to have a different task than the prosecution—an easier one.

The prosecution has to prove that Jenny is the killer, and they have to do so beyond a reasonable doubt. Our side, the defense, just has to show that their case is not ironclad; we don't have to prove that someone else did it.

In the real world that is this case; however, our burden is much greater. Because of the circumstances, the jury will view Jenny's guilt as likely, and the only way we will be able to refute that definitively is to demonstrate someone else's guilt.

To feel good about themselves, to feel like they have accomplished something, the jury will have to leave this trial believing that the guilty party will be punished for plunging a knife into Ryan Griffin's back. If that is not Jenny, then it will have to be someone else.

Our job is to find the someone else.

But we can't know who might have killed the victim until we know who the victim was. Hopefully we'll find out that the night before Griffin was killed he slapped a Mafia boss in the face, or publicly dared a serial killer to come after him. But I have the feeling the answer will be slightly more subtle than that.

Jenny has facilitated the investigative process a bit by making a phone call. The director of the film they were shooting in New York is a guy named Edward Markle. He's what Jenny describes as a mid-level director, meaning he's talented and gets regular work, but has never had a breakthrough hit.

The film is being shut down for obvious reasons, and Markle will be heading back to Los Angeles. Jenny called him and asked if he would meet with me before he left, and he agreed. Apparently he and Jenny were emotional allies against Griffin, who was by all accounts obnoxious to everyone on the set.

He's got a noon flight from Newark Airport, and we make arrangements to meet in an airport restaurant at 9 A.M. It's obviously a place located before the entrance through security, since I don't have a plane ticket. I'm hoping not to have to need one, but I'm starting to be afraid that is going to be wishful thinking in this case. Still, I'm really hoping I won't have to go to California.

Newark Airport used to be simple to get in and out of, and then the planners took over. Now there is a bewildering maze of roads to navigate reaching the place. I thought that my GPS, when I set it as my destination, would ask me in disgust if I wouldn't rather go to JFK or LaGuardia.

But I was just there driving Ricky to his teen tour departure, so I'm an old hand at knowing my way around. I get here early, but Edward Markle is still waiting for me when I arrive.

He's got an unusual look about him. He's probably sixty years old, with gray hair pulled into a pony tail. Think Kenny Rogers in a Dodgers sweatshirt and Lakers cap. But he manages to pull off the whole thing while appearing conservative, rather than like an aging hippie.

I grab a coffee at the counter and join him at the table. "Thanks for seeing me," I say.

"Anything for Jenny."

"You're good friends?"

He shakes his head. "No. I met her a couple of times before this shoot, but she's good people. No doubt about that. And

I can't see her stabbing Griffin in the back, although I thought of doing it myself a few times."

"You and he didn't get along?"

"He was just a pain in the ass, at least on this picture. He was a decent actor, but he thought he was Daniel Day Lewis, you know?"

"Hard to control?" I ask.

"Yeah, especially since it was his show and his money. That's a bad combination when it comes to trying to direct an actor."

"Was this the first time you worked with him?"

"Yeah. I had heard mostly good things. But on this shoot he was stressed out, volatile. He was on something . . . maybe drugs, maybe power. I don't know."

"Did he ever talk about anything going on in his life?" I ask.

He shrugs. "Not to me; we didn't have that kind of relationship. He saw me as a hired hand. He was distracted a lot of the time, which I guess makes sense. He had a bunch of projects going on as a producer, and acting is a full-time job. I was planning to have a straight talk with him after the shoot. He had to cut back somewhere, so I was going to give him advice that I knew he would ignore."

"Did you get any insight into his relationship with Jenny?"

"Not really. I knew there was some history there, but there's no doubt she had moved on. There were rumors that Ryan was having an affair with somebody on the production, but I never tried to confirm that."

"It didn't affect his work?"

He shrugs. "I have no idea; I was just putting my head down and going one day at a time."

"Did Jenny know he was fooling around?"

"I don't know that either. But Ryan's attitude toward Jenny was different than toward other women. Jenny had some kind of hold on him. I just think Jenny had moved on; she couldn't wait for the shoot to be over, so she could get away from him for good. But that was just my impression; not anything she said."

"Is that how you felt? You wanted it to end?"

"Maybe, but I don't really think of things that way. It's a job; I show up for work and do what I have to do. I like what I do and I think I'm good at it, but I'm not Scorsese, you know? I do the best that I can and then move on."

"Did you know Jenny had told Griffin she was quitting the film?"

He is obviously surprised by this. "Really? That would have been a shit show. She must have been more miserable than I thought."

"So what are you moving on to next?"

"Not sure yet, but there will be something. I'm going to meet with my agent next week. With the streaming services, there's a lot of work to be had."

"And the film you were here to shoot is canceled?"

He smiles. "Yeah, I would say so. The producer is dead, and he was one of the leads. The other lead is in jail. The stars are not exactly aligning."

"Maybe it will find another producer and you can get different leads?"

He shrugs. "Could be. It's a pretty good script, so maybe someone will pick it up and recast it. Scripts never actually die in Hollywood; they play musical chairs. They circulate in the community, and when the music stops, they try to find a place to sit down. But I will have moved on."

"What will happen to Griffin's company and his other projects?"

Another shrug. "Beats the hell out of me. But I would guess the vultures are flying around it even as we speak."

While I still know very little about Ryan Griffin, I've already uncovered a number of areas to explore.

One is money; Griffin had a lot of it, and was probably representing investors who had as much or more. Money is often a cause of violence, mainly because everybody wants it. I don't know Griffin's actual financial situation, but it's certainly worth checking into.

Griffin was also a power player, at least in Hollywood and formerly in the financial community. Where there is power, there can often be someone looking to take that power away. A knife in the back can serve as a permanent power remover.

At least as interesting is Griffin's apparent involvement with drugs. There are very few pacifist drug dealers, so it's always possible that Griffin's connections in that world caused someone to have reason to harm him. At the very least, it is something for me to point to if I have to muddy the waters that the jury will be trying to navigate.

To that end, I call Laurie and ask her to give Marcus an assignment. My assumption is that Griffin had a drug contact in New York; I doubt he had the stuff FedExed to him from California. So I want to see if Marcus can find out who that contact was.

Less interesting as a motive for murder, but something that I cannot at this point dismiss out of hand, are the romantic relationships Griffin has had. According to Jenny, and for that matter the gossip magazines, Griffin was involved with quite a few women in recent times, and was not above cheating on them.

Sex and betrayal may not be as likely motives for murder as money, power, and drugs, but they're not far behind those things on the list. So we cannot discount it, at least not until we learn more. Our task is to find the real killer and prove that he or she is guilty.

Piece of cake.

I call Sam Willis and ask him to get me a list of investors in Causeway Capital. "It's a private company, so it might take some digging," I say. "They do not disclose it."

"I'm a really good digger," Sam says.

"I've heard that. I'm only interested in the investors that were there when Griffin was with the company. So any that came in after that don't matter."

"Got it."

"And if possible, I'd also like to know who invested in his movies. Hopefully some names will pop up on both lists."

"I'm on it."

Laurie is calling on the other line, so I get off the call with Sam and answer her. "Marcus has found the two security guys who were with Griffin that night," she says.

"Are they local?"

"Depends what you mean by local. . . . Marcus says they run a private security company in the Bronx."

"Has he talked to them?"

"No. He's waiting for instructions from you."

"We need to speak with them," I say.

"Yes, we do."

"You don't have to be there."

"Maybe not, but I'm going to be," she says. "Marcus, you, and

I can pay them a visit. They may be less than welcoming after the other night at Charlie's."

I'm not going to argue the point for two reasons. Number one, I would lose. Number two, I'd want to lose. Heading to the Bronx to meet two large, pissed-off security guys is not my idea of a fun time out on the town, even with Marcus. Laurie has demonstrated her value in situations like this on many occasions.

"Okay, but I want to do this quickly," I say. "Based on the discovery, it appears the cops don't know about these guys yet, so I want to talk to them first."

"Marcus says the best time is during the day; they have an office on Fordham Road."

"So when can we do it?"

"I'll have Marcus confirm that they're on-site, and we can go right away. You can come home and pick me up."

"I'm on my way," I say.

The last time I was on Fordham Road in the Bronx was to see a basketball game at Fordham University.

The fact that Fordham University is on Fordham Road must be one of life's great coincidences. Or not.

Fordham plays their games in Rose Hill Gymnasium, which was not exactly a name designed to intimidate opponents. Of course, I'm no one to talk; I went to NYU, whose team nickname is literally the *Violets*.

Master Security has a storefront in a strip mall about a mile from the university, between a Subway restaurant and a dollar store. There are no cars in front of it, but we park down at the opposite end, which is where Marcus is sitting in his car.

We get out, as does he. "Are they inside?" Laurie asks.

Marcus nods; his goal in life is to say as few words as possible.

"How many are there?" I ask.

"Three."

"Do we have a plan?"

He shrugs. "We'll go in."

"That doesn't sound too complicated," I say. "Let's go." The truth is that I'm surprised that Marcus hasn't formulated more of a plan. Even though he makes Superman look like a helpless wimp, he's usually careful, mapping out a strategy and anticipating potential problems. Maybe he has done so this time, but just isn't revealing it.

In any event, neither he nor Laurie seem worried, and since I am not exactly the crucial security piece here, I'll take their confidence at face value.

We walk down to the office and enter. There are two desks, two chairs, a couch, and some filing cabinets. Everything is cheap and bland; these are not guys who threw a lot of money at an interior decorator.

The two guys who were with Griffin at Charlie's the other night are both here. Jenny had said that she heard them referred to on the set as Danny and Gurley, but I don't know which is which, and at this point it doesn't really matter.

Business does not seem to be booming, as they are currently playing cards at one of the desks. Based on the position of the cards, I think they're playing gin. These are the kinds of things a crack investigator notices.

They both look up in surprise at the sound of the door opening; I don't think they get much street traffic here. One of them says, "Well, Danny, look who's here."

Because of my aforementioned investigative talents, I deduce that the one who is talking must be Gurley.

They both stand, and Danny yells out, "Hey, Ruben, we have guests."

After a few seconds, the third member of the trio, obviously named Ruben, comes in through a door behind one of the desks. Gurley and Danny are very large men, but Ruben probably has twenty pounds and three inches on both of them.

"Who are they?" Ruben asks, disdain obvious in his voice. For all he would know, we could be potential clients, in which case he's apparently not concerned about making a good first impression. I don't think they are actively soliciting new business.

"They're from the other night in Jersey," Danny says. "This one is the guy that got me from behind." He points to Marcus as he says it, and then turns to Laurie and me. "She twisted Griffin's arm, and he just has a big mouth."

Ruben walks over to Marcus and stands about five feet away from him, taking a challenging pose. "You like to attack people when they're not looking?"

Marcus doesn't answer or react in any way. But I say, "Guys, what happened the other night happened, it's over. We're just here to talk and get some information."

Nobody acts in any way as if they heard me. Which once again raises the age-old question: When a lawyer speaks in an office on Fordham Road and none of the goons listen, did he make a sound?

Ruben remains focused on Marcus. "Maybe you're not so tough when someone like me is standing right in front of you, huh?"

Again Marcus does not respond, so I try again. "Ruben, you should take what happened to these guys the other night as a learning opportunity. Do not take this past the conversation stage; it will not end well for you. I say that as a close friend."

Again I'm ignored. I look over at Laurie, who seems simultaneously alert and amused, but she doesn't say anything either.

Ruben keeps talking to Marcus. "Come with me, asshole. I'll show you the alley we have in back, and you can show me how tough you are."

"Ruben, your parents raised an idiot," I say, giving up on any attempt at conciliation. This time he glares at me and says, "You can be next." Then he turns toward that back door and Marcus follows him through it.

The four of us remaining in the office don't say anything; we just wait for the resolution of the dispute between the Moron Formerly Known as Ruben and Marcus. Unless Ruben has a marine battalion waiting in the alley to have his back, he is in major trouble. And even then . . .

We don't have long to wait. The door opens and Marcus comes walking through. He has an ankle in his hand, and for a moment I'm afraid he has detached it from Ruben. But he hasn't; he's using the ankle to drag the unconscious Ruben into the office.

Danny seems stunned, but Gurley reacts by reaching into his jacket. "No," says Laurie, and when Gurley and I look at her, she is holding a handgun in her hand, which is where handguns are meant to be. "Slowly take it out of your pocket and lay it on the floor."

Gurley does so, and Laurie says to Danny, "Now you."

"I'm not carrying," Danny says, but since he really hasn't earned our trust, Marcus goes over and frisks him to confirm. Sure enough, Danny was lying, and Marcus takes the gun and puts it in his own pocket.

"This was not necessary," I say. "Ruben could be conscious now. We really just want to talk."

"So talk," Danny says.

"How did Griffin get to the house where he was killed?"

"I don't know."

"Danny, your goal should be to be smarter than your friend Ruben. That is a very low bar to clear. So just tell the truth and we'll be on our way."

Danny and Gurley make eye contact, and Danny says, "We dropped him off. He said we should take off, so we did."

"Was anyone else there?"

"I think so. The lights were on, and I might have seen the girl through the window; I'm not sure. The house is far from the street."

This is not good news. "Have you told the police that?"

"We haven't talked to any cops," Gurley says, jumping in.

"What time did you drop him off?" I ask.

Gurley shrugs. "I don't know . . . two, maybe three hours after we left that sports bar."

"Who hired you to provide security for Griffin?"

"He did. We were just supposed to watch him."

That's a strange way to put it; Griffin hired someone to watch him? Not to protect him? Maybe to protect him from himself? "How did he find you?"

"He said he heard about us," Gurley says. "I don't know where."

"How much did he pay you?"

"Ten thousand a month."

"What else did he say when you were driving to the house that night?"

"Nothing; he didn't talk much." Gurley has taken over for Danny; he is now the spokesman.

"How was he planning to get home?"

"None of our business. He told us to leave so we left."

"How did he get in the house?"

"I just told you, we left," Gurley says. Then, "Maybe the girl let him in."

I've run out of questions, and I look at Laurie, who shrugs. So I leave them with one final statement. "Danny, Gurley, if we find out you lied about any of this, we'll be back. Please convey that to your friend Ruben when he wakes up."

Bondar watched from a distance while the three people were in the strip mall office.

He didn't know who they were, but he took photos of them coming out with a high-powered lens, and he also photographed their license plates.

That probably wouldn't be necessary to learn their identities; the three idiots who they were visiting would tell him. And they would certainly tell him what the visitors wanted; there was no doubt about that.

When Bondar wanted people to talk, they talked.

James Shaffer must have realized by now that I was not going to make the overture, so he has decided to call me.

"You want to come in and talk about where this case is headed," he asks, sounding like every prosecutor I have ever spoken to.

"It's headed for an acquittal," I say. "And I would hope a sincere apology from the state of New Jersey, along with maybe a flower arrangement for my client. Don't send vegetables, we've got that covered."

He laughs a fake laugh. "The state of New Jersey foresees a different outcome."

"That's so typical of New Jersey; it's not exactly the Einstein of states. But that's what trials are for."

"There doesn't necessarily have to be a trial. That's what plea deals are for. You want to come in and discuss it?"

I'm not surprised that Shaffer is offering to make a deal, though I suspect that he is just doing what his bosses want. They likely have different interests.

He thinks he has a winning hand in a case that will provide him with a national platform; he will become known and famous in a way that is truly a once-in-a-lifetime manner. He has confidence in both his own ability and the evidence, and he isn't worried about becoming the next Marcia Clark and Christopher Darden.

His bosses, however, would see a plea deal as a major win; they would get to put Jenny away and claim a triumph without going through the considerable expense of a trial and the slight chance of a humiliating loss.

Of course, I have no inside information here; my view of their motives is just my best guess. In any event, it doesn't matter. Jenny has already told me that she has no intention of admitting to a murder she did not commit.

"I don't see any great reason for me to come in, unless you're offering door prizes. So we can do this on the phone. What did you have in mind?" I ask, not because we would accept any deal he proposes, but rather to assess their level of confidence.

"There can be an argument that she killed an abusive boyfriend, so I can probably swing thirty years, followed by probation of ten more. But if we go to trial, it will be life. She did stab the guy in the back; pretty tough to portray it as a heroic act of self-defense."

"Actually, she didn't, and I don't recall us mentioning self-defense. If your offer was an hour and a half in jail, plus twenty minutes' probation, it wouldn't take her that long to turn it down."

"That sounds fairly definitive," he says. "But I'm obligated to give you forty-eight hours to think about it."

"Don't sit by the phone," I say. "See you at jury selection."

I sounded a lot more confident than I am, which is not particularly difficult to do at this point.

When I get off the phone I notice that the house smells much better than usual this morning. Ever the detective, I set out to find out why.

It turns out that Linda Ivers is here and baking cookies. Linda has been coming over periodically to help Jenny.

Jenny, probably to maintain her own sanity, is behaving as if she is going to come out of this with her career and life intact. So she's conducting business, dealing with her agent, getting and reading scripts, etc. Linda is facilitating everything, like a good assistant should.

But this cookie thing is above and beyond. A batch has already been made . . . oatmeal raisin, which is my favorite. So to be nice, I try one . . . wow.

"These are great," I say, truthfully.

"Thanks. I also made a batch without raisins so you can give some to the dogs as treats."

By doing that, she moved up in my unofficial rankings of humans that I know. Raisins are bad for dogs.

After sucking down a bunch of the cookies, I call Sam Willis and ask him to use his magic ability to *enter* the phone company's computers to track some numbers.

"I want to know anyone that Griffin called the night he died," I say. The cops are probably getting that information as well, and they'll turn it over in discovery, but just in case, we should have it.

"On it," Sam says.

"Do you have his cell phone number?"

"Andy . . ." he says, obviously insulted by the question.

"Also, there's a company on Fordham Road in the Bronx called Master Security. The two guys who were with Griffin at Charlie's the other night work there, or maybe they own it with a moron named Ruben."

"Okay, what about them?"

"I'd also like to learn whatever you can about the company, and who they called that night as well."

"All three of them?"

"If you can."

"I can. Anything else?"

"I also want you to find out who really killed Griffin, and tell me how I can prove it to the jury."

"How the hell can I do that?" he asks.

"You can't. I was on a roll, so I figured I'd take a shot."

'm going to have to go to Los Angeles.

On some level I've known that since this case began, but I've been denying it even to myself.

The last time I was out there was a number of years ago. Willie Miller and I went out to meet with the studio that had purchased the rights to Willie's story and trial. Willie had been on death row for a murder he did not commit, and I defended him on appeal.

We won the case, which is why the studio was interested enough to buy the rights. You can tell how well the meeting went by the fact that the movie didn't get made . . . not even close.

The studio executive told Willie that he wanted to create a new character, Willie's mother, who came to visit him every day for seven years and always believed in his innocence. In real life Willie's mother abandoned him when he was six months old, so Willie was not inclined to make her the hero of his story.

I considered the meeting a success just based on the fact that I had talked Willie out of throwing the executive out through his office window.

We were on the eighth floor.

This time I'll book the flights and hotels online myself when I figure out when to go. I would have Edna do it, but if I tell her I want to go to LA, she could wind up booking me to Louisiana, or Lake Arrowhead, or Latvia.

But first I've caught a break which will let me delay my trip for at least another day. I want to interview Griffin's ex-wife, Audrey Dodge, but when I mention that to Jenny, she says, "I'm sure Audrey is in New York."

"Why do you say that?"

"She was already here; she is one of the producers on the movie, and she's very hands-on about it. And I'm sure she wanted to be able to keep an eye on Ryan."

"Why? Did she have a thing for him?"

Jenny looks at me strangely. "You've never heard of Audrey Dodge?"

"No. Should I have?"

"What about Carl Dodge?"

"Sounds familiar, but I can't place it."

Jenny seems amazed by that. "Okay. Carl Dodge started as a studio executive and went over to the production side. He became extremely successful . . . I'm sure you've seen many of his movies over the years . . . and then used his money to branch out into the hotel business. You've heard of Vista Hotels?"

I nod. "That I've heard of."

"That's Carl Dodge. When the hotel business took off, he became even richer, much richer, and used that money to finance even more of his own movies. He became a template for Ryan Griffin to model himself after; when you use your own money it gives you total control.

"Ryan sought him out when he came to Hollywood, and Carl took him under his wing. Carl is getting way on in years now, and has stopped producing films. It was through Carl that Ryan met his daughter, Audrey, who had become a producer in her own right. Then Audrey and Carl had some kind of mega argument, and she never sees him or speaks to him.

"But Audrey and Ryan got married and did some projects

together. The one we were shooting was one of them. Audrey will have a lot to do now; it's complicated to pull the plug on a picture."

"So she and Ryan were friendly? Their split was amicable?"

She shrugs. "Always seemed that way to me, but you can never tell."

"Do you consider her a friend?"

She smiles. "We both experienced the whirlwind that was Ryan Griffin . . . of course she went through it a lot longer than I did. But the common experience brought us together; we shared the same foxhole."

"Did Audrey and Ryan have any kids?"

She shakes her head. "No. Ryan was adamant that he did not want children."

"Does she have a place in New York? I'm meeting her at the production offices."

Jenny shakes her head. "No, I think she's staying at the St. Regis. She thought about staying with me—I told her she could—but she's not really the quiet, suburban neighborhood type. She likes to be out and about."

Then Jenny asks me the question that 100 percent of my clients ask 100 percent of the time we talk. "Any progress on the case?"

"We're still in the learning phase," I say.

"How long does that phase last?"

"Until we know enough." Then, "How's the gardening going?"

"Very well. We just planted the kale this morning."

"I can feel my mouth starting to water."

The All Together Now production office is on Fifty-seventh Street, just east of Seventh Avenue.

It's not listed on the lobby directory, but a special makeshift sign directs visitors to the third floor. I suspect the reason for this is that the offices are temporary, though they no doubt have become even more temporary than originally expected.

There is no one at the reception desk, probably because there is no reception desk. When I get off the elevator I seem to already be in the office. There's nothing impressive about it; the furniture is bland and no doubt rented. It's a certainty that the set decorator on the film was not consulted.

There are a few people walking around; I wouldn't say aimlessly, but nor does it seem like they have any particular purpose. One of them carries a cardboard box and disappears with it through one of the doors.

A young woman asks, "Who are you looking for?"

"Audrey Dodge."

I think I detect a slight frown and eye roll, but I'm not sure. The woman just says, "Through that door and head for the yelling."

"Thanks." I go through the door, which brings me into a corridor with three doors along each side. I don't hear any yelling, which leaves me unable to follow the woman's directions.

Only one of the doors is open, so I head for that one. I look in, and there are two people in the office, a woman sitting behind the desk and a young man standing near her.

"Yes?" the man says.

"I'm looking for Audrey Dodge."

The woman behind the desk says, "Andy Carpenter?"

"That's me."

"Steve, will you excuse us for a few minutes?"

"Sure," he says, agreeably, though my sense is that he did not have a choice. He nods at me and walks by me on the way out.

I'm assuming the woman is Audrey Dodge, though she hasn't actually identified herself. She's probably in her midthirties, blond with some brown streaks in her hair, and tall, at least five ten.

She comes around the desk and shakes my hand. "I'm Audrey. Have a seat."

I sit on a chair and she sits on the couch, so I turn the chair slightly to face her. "Thanks for seeing me," I say.

She smiles. "No problem. Happy to help Jenny in any way I can, and anything that takes my mind off my job is a welcome respite."

"You're not enjoying your work?"

"Not these days. Making a movie is hard, but unmaking one is even harder."

"Why is that?"

"Well, there had been so much preparation that has to be unwound. Locations, contracts with vendors, deals with distributors . . . but the emotional part is the toughest."

"How so?"

"For one thing, many jobs are lost, people's livelihoods are affected. But a movie is a special thing; it's not like any product. So much goes into it. Edward has been working on this for almost two years; to just pull the plug on it is terribly upsetting."

She's talking about Edward Markle, the film's director, who I spoke to at Newark Airport. He hadn't seemed that upset.

She continues. "Directing a film is an extraordinarily intense experience that starts way before shooting. It's upsetting to me and I have other projects. This was Edward's baby."

"Was this the only project you shared with Ryan Griffin?"

She shakes her head. "No, there were a number of them."

"What will happen to those?" I ask.

"They should still happen; Ryan had a good team behind him, and his partner will take over. Of course, there were two films in which Ryan was going to act, and the parts will have to be recast. But life goes on," she says, and then catches herself. "Except in Ryan's case."

"Was your father involved with this film?" Jenny had described Carl Dodge as Ryan's mentor, and the obvious reason that Audrey Dodge became a producer.

She seems put off by the question and responds quickly. "No. He's retired."

"I'm told Ryan was acting somewhat erratically in the weeks before he died."

She nods. "He was. I tried to speak to him about it, but got nowhere. He told me I was crazy and imagining things."

"Could it have been drugs?"

"That's a pretty good bet," she says.

"What was Griffin's attitude toward Jenny?"

"He loved her, even more than was normal for Ryan. But in all cases, for Ryan, love was a temporary affliction. He would have gotten over Jenny eventually, but it was taking an unusually long time, maybe because she dumped him. He hated losing at anything."

"Was he abusive toward her?"

"Physically, you mean?"

"In any way."

"Not physically; that wasn't his style. Verbally, maybe."

I saw him grab Jenny's arm in an angry fashion at Charlie's, so I'm not sure if I believe what she's saying, even if she does. I just let her continue.

"Emotionally? Very possibly," she says. "If he didn't, then Jenny was the exception. But I honestly didn't know that much about their relationship, except for what Jenny would say. And she didn't like to talk about it much, which was fine with me."

"So why did women put up with it?"

"You mean why did I put up with it as long as I did?" she asks, but doesn't wait for an answer. "Because Ryan was the most charming, charismatic, irresistible person ever put on the planet. You could hate him one minute and love him the next." She smiles. "Jenny had somewhat less patience with him."

"You mean she broke it off quickly?"

She nods. "Yes, which must have driven Ryan crazy. He was used to being the one who walked away. But Jenny didn't take any of his crap; I just hope she didn't kill him."

"You think she could have?"

"Any woman who ever loved Ryan could have killed him. That was part of his charm."

found something interesting," Sam says. "You coming into the office?"

"I wasn't planning to; I'm on my way back from the city."

"Okay. I also have some names of investors in Causeway Capital that match up to investors in Griffin's movie ventures. I'll bring it over and meet you at the house."

"Perfect."

"Do you know if there are any of those oatmeal raisin cookies that Linda Ivers made left?" he asks. "They are unbelievable."

"I don't know, Sam. But if there are, and if the information you have for me is good, you can have one."

It's only after I hang up that I realize that he referred to the list of investors as something he also had, so I assume that wasn't what he was referring to as interesting. I could call him back and ask, but I'll find out soon enough.

Sam is in fact waiting for me when I get home, chomping on cookies. He's talking to Jenny with his mouth full; they seem to be arguing about whether or not the Lakers will ever win another championship. Sam is taking the *no* position, while Jenny is sure that next year will be the year.

"I have floor seats," Jenny says. "With any luck I'll get to sit in them again."

I tell Sam that I need to walk the dogs and ask if he wants to come along. "No, I'll wait here with Jenny," he says.

I don't want Sam spending time with Jenny, because I don't want him discussing the case with her. "Wrong answer; come with me."

Tara and Hunter, as always, are eager to go out and sample the world, even if that world is just Eastside Park. Sebastian is reluctant; reluctance is in Sebastian's DNA. But he also has become sort of fascinated with Mamie and doesn't want to leave her alone.

He stares at her constantly; I think he may view her as lunch, so I resolve not to leave them alone. I don't want to come into the room one day and find him picking white hairs out of his teeth.

Once we're outside and walking, I ask Sam if he brought the list of investors with him. "Yeah, I left it on your desk," he says. "There are three entities that invested in both Causeway Capital and Griffin Productions."

"Entities? Not people?"

"Definitely entities. They appear to be some kind of holding companies; one is based in the Cayman Islands, one in Singapore, and one in UAE. All three of those places make it extraordinarily easy to conceal money and business transactions."

"What does that say to you?" I ask. "That there's something crooked going on?"

"No way to know at this point. Legitimate businesses like secrecy also, and they'll often seek out places and tactics like that."

"Okay. You also mentioned something interesting; is this what you're talking about?"

"No. I checked into Master Security, that company on Fordham Road."

"What did you find out?"

"That it doesn't exist; at least it doesn't exist as Master Security. It's just a storefront, rented to an individual named Michael Hutzler. There's no record at all of a company by that name."

"If they are a security company, and we know they carry weapons, wouldn't they have to be licensed in some fashion?"

"Legally, yes. But no licenses exist; I checked."

"No mention of the three guys . . . Ruben, Danny, or Gurley?"

"None that I could find. Just Michael Hutzler."

"Did you check into him?"

"As much as I could. There does not seem to be an actual Michael Hutzler. Actually, that's not quite true. There are two of them in the tristate area. One is in a rest home in Stamford, Connecticut, and the other lives in Leonia."

"Maybe he's the one in Leonia."

"I doubt it. Leonia's Michael Hutzler is four years old."

"Do we know how the firm got paid? Was it from the film production? From Griffin himself?"

"You're missing the point, Andy. There is no firm; Master Security doesn't exist. It has no bank account and no employees. It doesn't take in money and it doesn't pay any out. As best I can tell, the only evidence of anything called Master Security is the sign over the door."

"How about the three stooges? Ruben, Danny, and Gurley? They must not be working for free," I say.

"I just started looking into that. Ruben's last name is Allegra, and he has a bank account with a current balance of a hundred and eleven thousand dollars."

"Wow. The company that doesn't exist must be doing really well. Where did he get the money?"

Sam shrugs. "For all I know, it's from the money fairy. All of his deposits were in cash, and all for just under ten thousand."

"To conceal them?"

"Right. Any cash transactions over ten thousand have to be reported to the IRS. I suspect Ruben is opposed to that rule."

"Doesn't make it criminal," I say. "But it's certainly interesting. See what else you can find out about our three tough guys."

"Will do," Sam says. "I'll stop by again when I know anything."

"You'll have to call me," I say. "I'll be in California."

I wish Laurie were coming with me, but she can't.

In addition to the Jenny Nichols case, she and her K Team colleagues are working on a cold case for the Paterson Police Department. So she was forced to decline my invitation to join me in LA, even though I promised to get her a map of the movie stars' homes and show her where the Brown Derby used to be.

I also wish Tara were coming with me, but the chance that I would put her in a crate in the bottom of an airplane is absolute zero. I know that between Laurie and Jenny, all the dogs will get treated like royalty while I'm gone, so I don't feel bad about that.

I explain to Tara exactly what is going on. She patiently listens but doesn't say anything, probably because she is a dog and can't talk. But she can understand things, that's for sure, and I can tell that she is pissed off at me for abandoning her. Just before I leave she takes a biscuit from me, but she does so grudgingly.

It's a little strange that I'll be in the same general area as Ricky, who is traipsing through the West with the teen tour. We've already heard from him three times, and he sounds great. One was a FaceTime call, which thankfully Laurie knows how to work.

The last time he called it was right after seeing the Grand Canyon, and he was suitably impressed. He seems to like the outdoors; when he gets home he'll probably start growing vegetables.

I don't think he'd be crazy about his father showing up to join him on the tour, so I will stifle the impulse.

I have a one o'clock flight this afternoon. Based on my record with previous flights, it can leave on time, or it can leave a week from Wednesday. When I arrive at the airport, the monitors say that it is on time, which may or may not mean anything. The truth is, I don't have a lot of faith in the airlines.

Security takes twenty minutes, which is better than usual. While on line, I notice a sign saying that passengers seventy-five years of age and older do not have to take off their shoes. That's a bit puzzling. Old people could not be suicide bombers? They have more to live for?

I'm flying up front in first class, which I always considered a bit risky, since planes don't back into mountains. My boarding pass says that I am in group 1, so I'm standing in the front ready to board, thinking group 1 is the first group.

Not even close.

First on the plane are those in wheelchairs; there are three such people, and I don't begrudge them for going ahead of me. Next are those vaguely needing extra time to board. There seem to be no criteria to establish who those people are; it must be on the honor system. A whole parade of time needers walks by me, a few of whom look like they could be heading to compete in a decathlon event.

Next are passengers with little children; based on the number of those, I must be traveling with a preschool field trip. Then come members of the military; it turns out there are so many here that the best-defended place in the world must be gate 37 at Newark Airport.

By the time they call group 1, the plane is half full. But the flight does leave on time, and is quite pleasant. I find myself sitting in a reclining chair, watching television and eating peanuts and pretzels . . . a fulfilling existence that mirrors my life at home.

The only real difference is that I'm sitting next to a stranger instead of a golden retriever, and I don't think I should pet his head.

The flight is perfectly fine and comfortable, but for some reason I'm still exhausted when we land. I don't think I would have made a good wagon train guy.

If there was a before and after ad for an airport design company, LAX would be the before. It's an oval-shaped mess, overcrowded and set up in such a way as to have ridiculous traffic around the clock. The van ride to the car rental area seems to take almost as long as the flight, without the television, peanuts, and pretzels, but with plenty of strangers.

Unlike New York, which gives its highways names, like the Henry Hudson Parkway and FDR Drive, Los Angeles just uses numbers. I get on the 405; if they were to give it a name, an apt one would be the Marquis de Sade Freeway.

The traffic is ridiculous; it makes the roads at LAX seem like the Daytona Speedway. But finally I make it to the Fairmont Hotel in Santa Monica. It overlooks the Pacific Ocean, and even though I am tired and cranky, I have to admit it's a nice-looking hotel and a great-looking ocean.

A valet person takes my car. One thing I remember from my last time here is that there is valet parking everywhere. If they ever banned it, the unemployment rate in LA would go up to 50 percent. LA functions on a caste system with two classes—the people who physically park cars, and the people who don't.

I check in and before I know it I am in my room, which is actually a bungalow in the gardens. It's large and quite nice, a duplex with a terrific view; I could get used to this. Within a few minutes my eighty-five-dollar room service dinner is being delivered. I would use the minibar, but based on the prices, I probably need to be preapproved for a loan to do so. Do they give mortgages for macadamia nuts?

There must be a God, because the Dodgers are playing the Mets tonight, so I can settle in, watch the game, check in with Laurie, and then fall asleep.

Unfortunately, my long-dormant work ethic kicks in. I've brought discovery documents with me, so I start going through them for the second of what will be many times. When I get to the end of the forensics section, I'm so depressed that I stop and turn to the game.

The last thing I remember before falling asleep is missing Vince Scully.

Jenny Nichols may be stuck gardening at my house with an electronic ankle bracelet, but she still has power in Hollywood.

Maybe they're foreseeing the day when she comes back as a bigger star than ever, or maybe they just like her.

But phone calls from her have cleared the way to see most of the people I want to see out here; without that it's unlikely I would get anywhere. Amazingly I, Andy Carpenter, am not considered a celebrity in Hollywood.

Of course, no one who is anyone in Hollywood actually lives or works in Hollywood itself. My first stop today is in Century City, which is a collection of office towers with a shopping mall, theater, and hotel thrown in.

It's not far from the Fox studio lot on Pico, but Century City is best known to Americans as the location of the office tower in which a barefoot Bruce Willis defeated Alan Rickman and his bunch of ruthless terrorists in *Die Hard*. Just being here makes me start humming "Let it Snow."

Since Adam Milstein works at a place called The Milstein Agency, I suspect he didn't have to go through a grueling interview to get the job. His office is on the seventeenth floor of a modern office tower on Century Park East.

A security guard in the lobby has to call up to confirm that I have an appointment, and once that's accomplished, I head up, and when I get off the elevator, a man is standing there. "Andy Carpenter," he says, holding out his hand.

"That's my name also," I say, shaking his hand.

He laughs, more heartily than the joke called for, and invites me back to his office. I don't see anyone else along the way, which is not surprising, since except for the reception desk, there is no place for other people to work. This is a small shop.

His office is spacious, though, and it has a great, glass wall view heading west. I can see the Fox lot, and past that heading out toward Santa Monica and the Pacific. Someone with the Hubble Telescope could probably consider this office as having an ocean view.

He offers me something to drink, and I accept a Diet Coke. "I must say, the last person I expected to get a call from was Jenny Nichols," he says, smiling.

"Why?"

"Just because of all that's happened. I've always liked Jenny; I hope she didn't do this."

"She didn't. Jenny tells me that you were Ryan Griffin's agent?"

"In a manner of speaking."

"What does that mean?"

"Well, it was that rare job that paid no money, but that every agent in town eventually would have killed for."

"You Californians talk cryptically."

He laughs. "I grew up on the West Side of Manhattan."

"You transplanted New Yorkers talk cryptically."

"Sorry. I'll start at the beginning. Ryan Griffin came out here, already rich and successful, with the dream of being an actor. A friend had recommended me to him, and we hit it off, so he hired me to be his agent. I beat out a total of zero other agents to get the job.

"I got him a couple of parts, nothing huge, but not bad. One had a decent theatrical release, the other went straight to a DVD player near you. Ryan was fine in them; he was a pretty talented guy. He wasn't De Niro, but with training he could have had a good career. He would have been excellent in romantic comedies, very charismatic and women loved him. Think Hugh Jackman."

"People say I remind them of Hugh Jackman."

"You need to hang out with more honest people," he says. "But anyway, Ryan decided that with all his money, he didn't want to compete for acting jobs. He wanted to produce movies and since he was financing them, he would have total control. Which of course included casting."

"So he could give himself parts that appealed to him," I say, because my role is pointing out the obvious.

"Right. Which did not exactly leave a lot of need for my services. It would be a little ridiculous to negotiate a deal for Ryan Griffin the actor with Ryan Griffin the producer. But all of a sudden agents started swarming, wanting him as a client."

"Why did they become interested?"

"I'm a small shop; not that many clients. Enough for me to go to any restaurant I want, but not to get the best table. These other agents, the ones who wanted to take Ryan on, they have plenty of clients. And he was producing so many movies that they knew they could put their other clients in the films. It's called packaging."

"Meaning they control the whole package," I say.

"Exactly. They could even have their clients direct the films. But Ryan stuck with me, not out of any great sense of loyalty, but because he didn't want to be limited at all. He wanted to be able to hire people from anywhere. It made sense for him."

"He was becoming an important producer out here?"

Milstein laughs, though I didn't realize I had said anything funny. "Yes, with the kind of money he was spending, and the number of projects he had going, he was getting more important every day.

"You probably heard the joke; it's said about a lot of businesses, but it's particularly true about the film business: The quickest way to become a millionaire is to start out as a billionaire and self-finance movies. When someone like Ryan comes out here with all that money to spend, the vultures line up in flight formation."

"So nobody that you know would have been a candidate to kill him?"

"No chance. It was a dark day for the vultures when he died."

Ryan Griffin lived two lives, or at least had two careers. They weren't simultaneous, though they were connected by money.

Sometimes I think there is not much in life that isn't in some fashion connected by money.

Griffin had his New York financial career. He was a major hedge fund player, and if he wasn't at the top of that field, he was in shouting distance.

He went west to follow a dream, something he had always wanted to do. I can relate to that. I have often considered leaving the law to become quarterback of the New York Giants, and still might do it one of these days.

So he moved into his California/movie industry life, and by all accounts he was thriving in that as well. Certainly he bought his way in, which gave him a huge leg up. But that is not unprecedented, and certainly not frowned upon out here. As far as I can tell, this is an industry in which creativity is appreciated and nurtured, but money and power are cherished.

But I'm not here to dissect or critique Hollywood; any place responsible for both *Seinfeld* and *The Godfather* cannot be all bad. I'm here to learn about Ryan Griffin . . . who he was, what he did, and most important, who might have wanted him dead.

I stop for lunch before my next meeting at a place called The Lobster on Ocean Avenue in Santa Monica near the pier. I can picture the meeting they had to decide on the name for the restaurant. *We're going to serve lobster, so what should we call it? Wait . . . I've got an idea.*

I'm midway through my lobster roll and crab fried rice when Sam Willis calls to update me on my request to find out who Ryan Griffin called on the night he was murdered.

"There were seven calls," he says. "Two were to his own house in Los Angeles; I don't know if anyone was living there, or maybe he was just retrieving messages. Three were to Jenny Nichols; one would have been about an hour before she left for the party at Charlie's, and two while she was there. They were short; probably went to voice mail."

I remember at Charlie's that night that Jenny ignored two calls, and finally shut down her phone so she would stop being bothered. Those must have been the calls from Griffin.

"The sixth was to the Warwick Hotel on Fifty-fourth Street; obviously I have no way of knowing who he was calling or what it was about.

"The seventh one is a bit of a problem; it's got a country code of three-seven-five, which is Belarus."

"He called a number in Belarus? At what time?"

"Nine thirty P.M. eastern, which is five thirty in the morning in Belarus; they are eight hours ahead."

"How long did the call last?"

"Eight minutes."

"Can you find out who the phone is registered to?"

"Probably, but it might take a while. I haven't spent much time trying to penetrate the Belarus phone company."

"Could the phone have been in the US when he called it?"

"Of course. It could have been anywhere. The number doesn't change."

"Can you find out where that phone is now? Using that GPS

thing you do? Even though it's a foreign phone?" Sam has the ability to go into the phone company's computers and track the location of a phone through its GPS signals.

"I don't see why not," he says. "As long as it is connected into our tower system. Every phone has an IMEI number."

"I have no idea what that is, Sam, and I don't want to know. Please try to find it."

"Okay, but if it's not here, it may take me a while to learn that. It's like trying to prove a negative."

"Do your best. Thanks, Sam."

"You see any movie stars out there?"

"Not yet. But I'm going to a party at Sandra Bullock's house later, so there should be some there."

"Seriously?"

"Bye, Sam."

I feel bad about lying to Sam, even if it's an obvious one. The truth is that there is no way I am going to Sandra's house tonight; the Mets are playing the Dodgers again and I am not going to miss it. I'm going to tell Sandra the truth; she and Jennifer Aniston can always tell when I'm lying.

But before the game I go from one restaurant to another. I'm meeting Holly Knapp, who I'm told has become a significant person by accumulating something just under money and power on the list of things that industry people crave.

Information.

According to Jenny, Holly Knapp worked for *The Hollywood Reporter,* an industry magazine that is the main rival for *Variety,* the longtime leader in Hollywood journalism. She was hired as a reporter right out of journalism school, and was assigned basic, low-level stuff.

But Knapp apparently had a way about her that is rare, a personality that gets people to open up to her. Actors, producers, and executives don't only talk to her about what their next projects will be; they also confide about things in their private life.

So she started writing a column that was just biting and informative enough to get people to want more, but not to hate her for writing it. And then they started to be a little afraid of her, fearing what she would say about them, and also what she wouldn't. So that got them to talk to her even more, so that maybe they could have some control over the message.

Since Knapp is apparently just as smart as she is resourceful, it didn't take long for her to decide that she could do better than the salary she was making at the magazine. She figured she could start her own operation, be her own boss, and make far more money. All without changing anything that she was doing.

So she left and started producing a four-page paper that she came out with twice a week. It was even better than her work for *The Hollywood Reporter* had been, because she was free of any constraints. She writes what she wants, and the community has been eating it up.

We're meeting at Art's Deli on Ventura Boulevard in Studio City in the San Fernando Valley. On the way here, the car thermometer kept going higher and higher, amazingly so. I expected to pass a sign telling me that the equator was three miles up the road.

When I get out of the car I am stunned at how hot it is; I'm surprised that all the cars haven't sunk into the melting pavement.

But Art's is mercifully air-conditioned, and when I walk in, Holly Knapp is slurping up a bowl of soup. The restaurant is mostly empty, since three o'clock in the afternoon is not prime lunchtime. The person at the reception desk points her out to me, and when I walk over to her she waves with her left hand while using the soup spoon with her right. There is no wasted effort here.

"Andy?" she says as she takes the last mouthful. It comes out as something of a gargle, but I can make out the word.

"That's me."

"Minestrone is truly the perfect food. Someone could live on it and nothing else."

"That would be something of an empty existence."

"You don't like vegetables?"

"Are you kidding? We grow our own on the farm back home in Paterson."

"You have a farm?"

I nod. "Quite a spread; cement as far as the eye can see. Actually, Jenny is currently doing some of the farming."

She smiles, but then turns serious. "You have got to help her. This is all bullshit."

"Yes, it is."

"Jenny is one of my favorite people in Hollywood."

"Is there a long list?"

"You'd be surprised. People in this industry are no better or worse than anywhere else." She shrugs. "Not that I've been anywhere else. Now, how can I help?"

"Tell me what you can about Ryan Griffin."

"What do you know so far?" she asks.

"The abridged version is he was rich, charismatic, something of a womanizer, a reasonably talented actor, and he was buying his way to becoming a big-time producer by using his own money."

"You buried the lead," she says. "The key is the last part. You see, there is one superpower out here; the power to green-light. Everything else is in second place."

"You mean to say an absolute yes to a movie being made?"

"Right. And Ryan had that power; very few people outside the big corporations do."

"So he was active?"

She thinks for a few moments. "I'm going to give you something. . . . I was going to write about it, but . . . Ryan Griffin was going to create his own streaming service."

"You mean like Netflix?"

She nods. "Yes. A lot smaller, obviously, but you can't succeed in that world unless you are big. That's a fact."

"That would take huge money," I say.

"That's for sure. Did you know Netflix spends more than fifteen billion dollars a year on content? That's *billion* with a *b*. Those services are transforming this world. Ryan would not have been able to compete without enormous resources."

"All his money?"

"I have no idea, but I can't imagine it was. He had to have deep-pocketed investors."

"Do you know who they were?"

"No, but I've been trying to find out."

"Who would know?"

She shrugs. "I would say Arnold Chrisman."

"I've heard the name."

"He worked with Ryan. He's a lawyer, but pretty much handled all the internal stuff. More like a partner, but since Ryan had the money and the vision, Arnold was in second position."

"Can you get me in to see him?"

She smiles. "No chance. Arnold wouldn't piss on me if I were on fire."

"Why?"

"I wrote a couple of things about him that were accurate but unflattering."

"Did Ryan feel the same way about you?"

She laughs. "Not hardly."

"He was interested in you?"

"Let's say I was on his very long target list. But Jenny was at the top; she was different. He was obsessed with her. Not that you could blame him."

I just realized that I could tell Holly that I dated Jenny in high school; then she could write about it and the whole world would know. But as Jenny's lawyer, I don't think it would look great, so I'd better not.

Dammit.

Ruben was nervous; Danny and Gurley were not. That's because Ruben was smarter.

Sergey Bondar had called Ruben the previous day and arranged the meeting. He did not say much; Bondar never did. He just said that he had another job for them, and he designated a time and place for them to meet.

So the three men were waiting for Bondar at 9 P.M. in a wooded area in Suffern, New York. It was obviously a public park that had fallen into disrepair; there were still long unused swing sets and a small merry-go-round that children once played on.

Ruben had spent the last day trying to consider in his own mind whether Bondar might have reason to betray them. The fact that Ryan Griffin was murdered while theoretically on their watch was an obvious concern, but they had done nothing wrong.

Ruben assumed that Bondar had actually killed Griffin himself. It takes a special type of person to put a knife into someone's back, and Ruben had no doubt that Bondar could do such a thing without hesitating. Ruben did not know Bondar very well, but doubted there was anything Bondar would not do.

Danny and Gurley, for their part, took the situation at face value. They had never made as much money in their life as they had for the Griffin assignment, and they were eager for another, similarly lucrative job.

Ruben's nervousness was tempered by the fact that all three men could handle themselves. He was personally armed and ready for any eventuality, and if Bondar tried anything, he would more than have his hands full. But Ruben did not expect it would come to that.

Bondar was twenty minutes late when his pickup truck pulled up to where they were standing. It was very dark there; the only light was from the moon, and clouds diminished its effect. Bondar turned off his truck lights, but left the parking lights on so they could see.

Bondar got out of the truck and dispensed with the pleasantries. The three men didn't even see the handgun he was carrying, but within fifteen seconds of his arrival, Ruben and Danny were dead, both from a single shot in the chest.

It was an amazing display of marksmanship that Ruben and Danny did not get a chance to appreciate. Had they lived, they might have been flattered to know that Bondar chose them to be the first to die because he considered them the smartest, or at least smarter than Gurley.

"No . . . come on, no . . ." Gurley pleaded, his hands held in front of him in a defensive gesture, as if they could deflect any bullets coming his way.

"Relax, Gurley. Those guys screwed with me," Bondar said. "I know you weren't in on it."

"What did they do?"

"I just told you. They screwed with me. Now we need to dig their graves. I've got shovels in the truck."

Gurley had no idea what to make of what Bondar was saying, but he wasn't in a position to argue. He took one of the shovels and walked toward an area behind some trees. He and Bondar each dug a hole big enough for one of the bodies.

Gurley thought of trying to make a run for it; he certainly

didn't trust Bondar. But he knew that Bondar would react quickly and shoot him before he got anywhere near his car. So he dug . . . and hoped.

When they were done, they went back to get the bodies, which now defined the term *dead weight*.

Gurley grabbed Danny under the arms, while Bondar did the same with the larger Ruben. Gurley noticed that Bondar had no trouble lifting Ruben off the ground, while Gurley had difficulty even dragging Danny. Bondar was incredibly strong.

Once the bodies were lowered into the ground, Gurley asked, "Can I go now?"

Bondar smiled. "You don't enjoy my company?"

"It's not that. I . . ."

"Let me ask you a question, Gurley. Three people came to see you at the office in the mall. Two men and a woman. What did they want?"

It took a few moments for Gurley to remember what Bondar was talking about. "Oh. One of them was a lawyer. He was working on the Griffin thing."

"I asked what they wanted."

"To know what happened that night. To know what we did."

"What did you tell them?"

"That we dropped Griffin off at the house and we left. And that we didn't know what happened after that."

"Was that the truth? Do you know what happened after that?"

"No."

"Did these people mention my name?"

"No."

"Did you?"

"No. I swear."

"Did you get their names?"

"Just the lawyer; his name is Carpenter."

Bondar did not know if Gurley was telling the truth; he suspected he was, but it didn't matter. The three of them had one job to do, and they botched it.

Worse than that, during the course of their time watching Griffin, they could easily have heard things that they weren't supposed to. With the lawyer now aware of their involvement, they could be questioned further, by the lawyer or the police.

Their inclination could be to talk and save themselves, which is why he had killed Ruben and Danny. It is also why he shot Gurley in the chest and set about digging a third grave.

s it proper to tip a valet person when they take your car, or only when they bring it back?

These are the kinds of questions that haunt me.

In the past I've always done it both times, but when I pull back up to the hotel, I'm behind two other cars, and neither of the drivers tipped the guy.

Have I been overdoing it my whole life? I've valet parked a lot of times . . . going back many years. All that money, earning interest, compounded quarterly . . .

I could be rich by now, although since I am actually already rich enough, I'm not going to obsess about it. And I still tip the guy when he takes my car, because Andy Carpenter is all about goodness and generosity.

I go through the lobby and out toward my bungalow. I have to admit that I like this bungalow thing; maybe I'll put one in the backyard back home, with a view of the vegetable garden. I could have the nicest and only bungalow in all of Paterson.

I'm about to enter when I stop short. . . . A small jolt of fear goes through my body. I'm a coward, so my body is used to fear jolts.

Laurie taught me something a couple of years ago. She did it for two reasons; one, because my life always seems to be in jeopardy, and two, because I often have material with me related to my case that is confidential and potentially valuable to adversaries.

What she taught me was to take a very small piece of scotch tape and put it vertically in the crack between the door and the wall. If it's undisturbed when I get back, all is good. If not, I could have a problem.

I have a problem.

The tape has obviously been moved; there's no question about that. It almost certainly could not have been a member of the hotel staff doing their job because I left a DO NOT DISTURB sign on the door, and signs like that are usually respected.

The door lock does not seem to have been tampered with, but I'm not exactly an expert in door lock tampering.

So now I have a decision to make. I can venture inside and see if there was an intruder and if that intruder is still there, waiting for me.

The other option is to go back to the desk and ask for security to accompany me inside. That would result in some humiliation and silent mocking if I was wrong about there being an intruder at all.

I head for the desk.

I tell the person at reception that I think there's a chance my room was broken into. She clearly doesn't believe there is any possibility that I am right, but does the right thing and calls security.

A decent-sized guy shows up a few minutes later. "You're not armed," I say.

"Do I need to be?" he asks.

"If there is an intruder in my room, it might come in handy."

He shrugs. "We'll just ask him to leave."

On the way to the bungalow, he asks why I think the room was broken into, and I deflect the question. "I'm probably crazy, but I've had a bad experience before, and I want to be sure."

He looks carefully at the door knob and lock before entering and just shrugs. I assume he doesn't see anything amiss. We enter, and all seems quiet. The room has not been made up by the chambermaid; the DO NOT DISTURB sign was effective.

After we look around downstairs, I ask him if he'd go upstairs to confirm that the coast is clear, and he frowns but does it. When he comes down, he says, "I think you're safe."

"Thank you. Are there security cameras that cover the entrances to these bungalows?"

"There are security cameras everywhere," he says.

He leaves, obviously to tell everyone in the hotel about the clown in bungalow seven. And he's probably right about that; I'm beginning to believe that I didn't put the tape on correctly, or securely.

And then I look at the desk.

The folder with the discovery documents that I read through last night is where I left it, open as it was when I stopped reading. But it's turned to the wrong page. I know for a fact that I stopped reading at the end of the forensics section, but the page facing me now is two pages later.

There is no chance I left it that way.

I call Laurie and tell her what happened.

"I don't like this," she says.

"I guess it's possible I could be wrong."

"What does your gut say?"

"My gut, as you know, is gutless, but it clearly believes I am right."

"I think you should come home."

"Come on, let's not overreact here."

"There's something else; Sam found it."

"What is it?"

"He's been looking into the financiers for Griffin's operation and films. It's a hard nut to crack, but he's learned that one of the largest investors comes through the hedge fund where Griffin had been a partner, Causeway Capital."

"No surprise."

"He hasn't been able to learn who those investors are, but he found something else very disturbing. A guy named Larry Hoffman was in charge of the entertainment assets at the fund; his title was managing director. So he would likely have been the person dealing with Griffin, or Griffin's people."

"He *was* in charge of the assets? Not anymore?"

"Not since he was killed in a hit-and-run accident on First Avenue four months ago."

didn't get much sleep last night, and it wasn't because it took me a while to finish arguing with Laurie about whether I should return home right away.

I sort of won that argument, in that after I promised to be careful, she was forced to give in. I also agreed to speak to the cops about what happened, but I was planning to talk with them anyway, so that was an easy concession to make. She said that either she or Corey would set it up.

And it wasn't because I moved into the main area of the hotel; the person behind the desk was surprised that I wanted to, and shocked that I was willing to pay the same room rate, even though the bungalows are more expensive. I packed up and was out of the bungalow within twenty minutes of getting off the phone with Laurie.

It was because the experience was unsettling; I could have been in the room when they broke in, and that likely would not have ended well. I also have no idea why they did it, but the fact that they went through the discovery documents but didn't steal anything makes me realize that it was not a random break-in.

I was the target.

I had asked the assistant manager if I could get a look at the security tapes for that area, but he told me that was against hotel policy.

"You're familiar with that policy because a lot of guests make the same request?" I asked.

He ignored that question and told me that law enforcement would have to make the request, and then the hotel would no doubt comply, but the decisions would be made above his level.

I could have pushed it, but I didn't, because I had another idea.

"Talk to me," Sam said as always, when he picked up on the first ring.

"Sam, the video that a hotel security camera takes . . . where does it go?"

"What do you mean?"

"I mean, is it in a disc in the camera, or does it get sent to the hotel's computers?"

"It's not in the camera, Andy . . . these days that's only true of consumer model cameras. An operation like a hotel, it would be sent to their computer system, probably wirelessly."

"Could you access it?"

"I don't see why not."

I give Sam the name of the hotel, the fact that it's a camera covering bungalow seven, and the hours I want him to look for. "If you find anyone going to that bungalow and entering, can you make a copy of it and send it to me?"

"Will do," he says. "So how is it in Hollywood?"

"What do you mean?"

"I've always wanted to go out there. Not just because of the movie stars; there are also a lot of things to do."

"Like what?"

"Like the La Brea Tar Pits. Have you been there? That is un-believably cool."

"I'm not here on vacation, Sam. But why is it cool?"

"All those dinosaur bones buried there . . ."

"Sam, let me tell you something about Hollywood. Everyone comes out here with a dream of stardom, but very few get there. For every T. rex that hit it big back in the day, there were a hundred that didn't make it, and they're the ones in the La Brea Tar Pits. Why would I want to see the losers' bones? The stars all went to Jurassic Park."

Sam seems unimpressed with my dinosaur soliloquy, so I get back to the matter at hand. "Laurie told me about the hedge fund guy that got killed. Larry Hoffman."

"Yeah. According to newspaper reports, the police think he might have been targeted because of the way it happened. Somebody caught the license plate number of the car that hit him. It was a rental car, and had been rented to someone with a fake ID. At least that's what the media had; Laurie is going to try to find out more from the local cops."

"Can you see if you can find any connection to Ryan Griffin in Hoffman's phone records?"

"Sure."

"Thanks. Let me know what you come up with."

"Did you go to Sandra Bullock's the other night? Or were you bullshitting me?"

"I was bullshitting you, Sam."

"That's what I figured. Sandra wouldn't give you the time of day."

'm surprised that Arnold Chrisman is willing to see me. Nobody set it up; I just called, spoke to his assistant, and got the word that Chrisman would meet with me this morning.

Griffin Entertainment, named for its deceased founder, occupies an entire building at the corner of Wilshire and Cloverfield in Santa Monica. It's a huge open space, with just a few executive offices along the outside walls.

It's got metal beams along the ceiling at odd angles and a corridor along the second floor that could double as a running track. It feels like the designer was making a statement, and that statement was *look how weird and creative we are*.

There's no reception desk; it seems like guests are supposed to wander around until they run into whomever they are here to see. In the center of the room is a man in his thirties, dressed casually in a sweater and khaki pants, who is addressing maybe twenty people in a circle around him. In this group, he is actually overdressed.

I can't hear what he's saying, but it looks like some kind of pep talk of sorts, but quite serious. I'm guessing that things have not been a lot of fun around here lately, since their leader and boss wound up dead on a kitchen floor.

The man in the center looks over and sees me; he raises his hand in a gesture that seems to suggest he'll be right with me, so I stop walking around the edge of the building and just stand there. After two or three minutes, the meeting breaks up and he walks toward me.

"You're Carpenter, right?"

"It's nice to be recognized."

"Let's go to my office."

That seems like a reasonable suggestion so I follow him to an office on the other side of the building. I look in the other offices as we pass them, and it turns out his is no different from theirs. This place is not about the trappings.

As we enter he says, "I've got water, flavored water, and flavored carbonated water."

"None of the above," I say. Just because I'm in California, it doesn't mean I am going to abandon my principles and start being health conscious.

"My wife said I shouldn't talk to you," Chrisman says.

"Really? I'm usually really popular with wives."

"You're representing the person who killed Ryan."

"Apparently the *innocent until proven guilty* concept hasn't worked its way west?"

"It's probably somewhere over Nebraska at this point," he says.

"So why did you disregard your wife's wishes?"

"I guess I'm just curious. Plus at the end of the day I don't see Jenny Nichols putting a knife in anybody's back, though in this case there would be some irony to it."

"How so?"

"Ryan had a reputation . . . never mind . . ."

"As a back stabber himself?" I ask.

"Some would say that, though it was not my experience. So what is it you want to talk about?"

"How serious was Griffin's drug use?"

He seems taken aback by the question, which was my intent. "Who told you he was using drugs?"

"Enough people that it can be accepted as fact. How bad was it?"

He pauses for a moment, and then shrugs. "It was manageable, but increasing. A cause for concern, but not panic."

"Who was his supplier?" I ask. A drug dealer is always someone to point to in front of a jury as a possible guilty party.

"I have no idea. But with Ryan's kind of money, he wasn't meeting someone in a dark alley. You can be sure of that."

"Was it impacting his work?"

"Not really. Ryan was a big picture guy; he left the nuts-and-bolts stuff to me. And he was high-functioning. He never showed up for work impaired in any way; that simply was not his style."

"Where did his money come from?"

"Come on, you must be further along than that. The guy ran a big hedge fund."

"I'm not talking about his personal money. You have investors; he wasn't going to start a streaming service by writing a personal check."

Chrisman reacts; I believe I've touched a nerve. "What makes you think we were going to start a streaming service?"

"I'm a savvy investigator. So who are your investors?"

"You must be confusing us with a public company. They are required to reveal things like that; we are not."

"So we're just spitballing here, but what if someone gave Griffin a great deal of money to invest, and then discovered him taking drugs, behaving erratically, and pursuing a bullshit acting career instead of taking care of business?"

"Mr. Carpenter . . ."

"And in the interest of continued spitballing, suppose that person couldn't control him and saw the chance of his or her money going down the drain."

"So an investor stabbed him in the back? That is truly ridiculous."

"You're not getting into the spitballing spirit," I say. "Did you know Larry Hoffman?"

"Of course. Larry was . . . You're trying to connect Larry's hit-and-run death with Ryan?"

"Two people connected to each other, both murdered within a few months. Quite a coincidence."

Chrisman shakes his head in amazement at my even bringing Hoffman into the conversation. "You must be desperate."

"Way too early for desperation. That comes later, just before panic. It's a process."

"I see. But if you think Larry Hoffman getting hit by a car in New York is related to Ryan Griffin being murdered, you may not be as savvy as you think you are."

"No one is as savvy as I think I am."

I slept well last night because I wasn't in that bungalow.

My room is now on the seventh floor of the main building, and the only way in is through the one door. I had it locked, with the bolt turned, and with that metal bar thing in place to make it even harder to break in.

Knowing that a bad guy would have to come up the elevator, walk all the way down the corridor, and break through that door, I felt pretty secure. Just in case, I put the DO NOT DISTURB sign on the doorknob; I think that's something that the bad guy would respect.

Today is my last day here, which is fine with me. It's a nice enough place, but I don't feel at home here, possibly because it's not home.

It just feels strange. For one thing, it occupies two entirely different climate zones. When I met Holly Knapp in the Valley the other day, the thermometer in my car said it was a hundred and one degrees. I drove the thirty minutes back to Santa Monica, where it was seventy-four.

That is not normal.

Today I'm in Hollywood, the first time I actually have been in Hollywood since I came here to learn more about Hollywood. And I don't see the famous Hollywood sign, since the Hollywood sign is not in Hollywood.

This is a strange place. If a lawyer wanted to learn about

Paterson, New Jersey, he would come to Paterson, New Jersey. And if Paterson had a famous Paterson sign, it would not be in Passaic.

But I'm here to meet with LAPD sergeant Keith Rossiter. Corey Douglas set up the meeting through that special connective network that exists between cops everywhere.

I have no idea how they do it; it certainly doesn't exist in the legal profession. If I wanted to meet with a lawyer in Topeka, I'd have to look in the Topeka phone book, if phone books still existed.

Rossiter is in the fraud unit, with a specialty focusing on the entertainment industry. From what I hear, he must be one busy guy.

Unlike New Jersey cops, who religiously avoid being on time when I am supposed to meet with them, Rossiter is waiting for me when I arrive, having left instructions with the front desk to send me back to his office.

On the way back there I notice that it looks like every other police station I've ever walked through. The only real difference is that the cops here don't hate me yet.

Rossiter's office has the dimensions of an average-sized walk-in closet, so I take the one chair available as he sits behind his desk. I thank him for seeing me, but he starts off by saying, "Lieutenant Drummond says you're a pain in the ass."

I have absolutely no idea who Lieutenant Drummond is, but Corey Douglas must have mentioned it to whoever he spoke to on the cop chain, and they must have accurately passed it along until it got to Rossiter.

"That Drummond is some kidder," I say. "We go way back."

"He said he never met you, but he's heard stories."

"Really? We could be talking about a different Drummond. Tall guy, but sort of short?"

"So you're representing Jenny Nichols."

"I am, which is why I want to talk about Ryan Griffin. Someone other than my client killed him."

He frowns. "In your client's kitchen, with her knife."

"In the hands of a lesser attorney, those would be problematic facts."

"I have a cousin who worked for Jenny Nichols on two films; he says she's a good person. Which is why I'm talking to you."

"She is. So tell me anything you can about Ryan Griffin."

"Be specific," he says.

"Drugs."

"That's not my area, but I checked up, and there's no doubt he was using. Heavily, and getting worse."

"Any talk of his not paying his bills?"

"None, and it wouldn't make sense. Not only was he rich as hell, but he'd want to keep getting supplied. Stiffing those people would be counterproductive and stupid. No one I know thought of him as stupid."

"Where was he getting the money to make all these movies? I'm not talking about his personal money; I'm talking about outside investors."

"I can't help you with that; they're a private company and they keep that information locked up tight. But I have my suspicions."

"Suspicions are always welcome," I say.

"What do you know about Carl Dodge?"

"I talked to his daughter . . . Griffin's ex-wife and producing partner. I know he was a mentor of sorts to Griffin, and was a big-time producer in his own right. What else should I know?"

"A while back, and we're talking thirty years, Carl Dodge produced his first movie. It was called *The First One to Scream*."

"Never heard of it," I say.

"I'm not surprised. It was a horror movie, by all accounts not a very good one. But it made thirty-five million in 1980s dollars. Which was not half bad."

"So?"

"So the word was that he had gotten the money to make it from the Ricci family, specifically Angelo Ricci. Angelo Ricci was not someone you wanted to owe money to."

"Is Angelo still alive?" I ask.

"Not since 2001, when his forehead stepped in front of a bullet. Actually three bullets. But it was apparently common knowledge, though I wasn't around back then to confirm it, that Carl Dodge's continuing to occupy the planet depended on that movie making money, so he could make Angelo whole and repay the debt. If it's true, and I believe it is, then Carl Dodge had a lot of guts. But he wanted a career, and he got one."

"So he paid off Angelo, who was therefore a happy camper," I ask.

"Probably. But Dodge went on to produce a shitload of movies, which required a shitload of money, and he was always thought to be still tied into that world. It was mutually beneficial; the films did well, for the most part, so the investors did well."

"Where was Dodge getting his money once Angelo bit the dust?"

"Hard to say. Angelo had his successors, but the family lost power when the organized crime business took something of a downturn. By then Carl had plenty of money of his own, and had probably found other investors who wanted to jump aboard."

It's an interesting story that he's telling, and my ears always perk up when I'm in a conversation about organized crime, but I'm not getting any closer to anything that can help me. "How does this relate to Ryan Griffin?" I ask.

"I'm getting there. Griffin came out to Hollywood intent on calling his own shots, and willing to do it without studio money. The template for that was Carl Dodge, and Dodge took a liking to him. Dodge was getting way up in years, so he took Griffin under his aging wing."

"Could he be financing Griffin?"

"Seems unlikely."

"Why is that?"

"Well, first of all, Griffin is spending way beyond anything Dodge ever did. It's a new world now, and to compete the spending has to be on an entirely different level. Second, Dodge hasn't been seen in a couple of years; people say he's at the end of a downhill slide. Alzheimer's."

"Where does Audrey fit in?"

"Depends who you talk to. Carl introduced them, but then he's said to have had a falling-out with his daughter not long after that. They apparently have no relationship to speak of."

"So bottom line, was Ryan Griffin involved with the kind of people who would kill him?"

Rossiter shrugs. "Could be, but that's not going to help you."

It feels like Rossiter's goal in life is to say things that are un-helpful. "Why not?"

"Because he wasn't failing; he was on the rise. Why put all that money in and then kill off your investment?"

"That wasn't the answer I was looking for," I say. "What would you say if I told you my bungalow at the Santa Monica Fairmont was broken into?"

"Did you report it to the police?"

"No."

"Then I wouldn't say anything. But I'd ask why they did it. Was anything stolen?"

"They were interested in reading my documents on the Griffin murder. Either that, or they were trying to scare me."

"Did they scare you?" he asks.

"They did."

"Then mission accomplished."

The flight home was once again comfortable and uneventful. We landed at Newark fifteen minutes early, but the airline compensated for that mistake by taking a half hour to send the bags down.

Laurie is waiting for me on the front porch with Tara and Hunter. Sebastian apparently and characteristically chose to sit this one out. I get a great, affectionate greeting from all three of them.

This return makes me realize that Dorothy was wise beyond her years . . . there's no place like home, there's no place like home. On the other hand, while she was happy to be home, Toto was far from off the hook. I still want to know how that was resolved.

When I get inside, Sam is there, as is Linda Ivers. Jenny, Linda, and Mamie are in the den, so Laurie and I take Sam into the kitchen to talk. He's here to show us the security tape from the hotel.

"I'm sorry if the quality isn't great; you would think a fancy hotel like that would have better equipment," he says. The video is on his iPad, so we look over his shoulder to watch.

The whole thing lasts about a minute. There is a time stamp on the bottom, which says that it was taken at 1:38 P.M. We see a man in a sweatshirt, sweatpants, and hoodie walk up to the bungalow door, fiddle with the lock, and enter. It's impossible to see how he got the lock to open; it's possible he had an electronic pass key.

The time stamp jumps, but not that far, to 1:41 P.M., as the door opens and the man leaves. He walks confidently, without looking around and apparently unafraid of being observed. I don't know if anyone would have made anything out of it anyway; he could just have been the guest staying in that bungalow, although he was dressed pretty warmly for the outdoor temperature that day.

At no point could his face be made out; he seemed to have a knowledge of where the camera was, and was always turned away from it.

"That's it," Sam says. "I spliced the entrance and exit together, but they were only three minutes apart."

"Which tells us everything we need to know about the break-in," Laurie says.

I know exactly what she means. "They weren't looking for information at all. They just wanted us to think that they were."

"They were sending you a message by turning the pages on the desk," she says. "And they were trying to scare you."

"I'll email you both copies of this," Sam says.

"Thanks, Sam. What else have you got?"

"A bunch of things—some are a work in progress, and one I've gotten nowhere on."

"Start with the nowhere one."

"I've looked further into the three entities that invested in both Causeway and Griffin's production company. Like I told you, they are based in the Caymans, Singapore, and the UAE. The secrecy is too tight and everything is shielded; I can't get any names to attach to them."

"You've taken it as far as you can?"

He nods. "It's a cyber brick wall. Believe me."

"Let's move on to the work in progress."

"Good . . . you'll like this. The Belarus phone number that Griffin called the night he died is in the name of Sergey Bondar. There's a Google mention that says he is wanted for murder by Interpol in Germany."

"So he's in Germany now?"

"I don't know. I haven't found the phone in the US yet, but that doesn't mean it isn't here. It's very difficult to do that tower search, but I'm working on it. But I found out something else interesting about him."

"What's that?"

"I looked for any trace of him in the Caymans; it's easier to search there than in Singapore or the UAE. Except for the financial side, it's a much more open society."

"And?" Laurie asks, trying to move this along. Sam has a tendency to dole out information slowly.

"He's been in the Caymans at least three times in the last year," Sam says. "Could be more, but I only found three."

"It would be good to know if he's here."

"I wouldn't be surprised if he is, because that security guy from the Bronx called the same number the day before Griffin died."

"Which security guy?"

"Ruben. As I mentioned, his full name is Ruben Allegra. He's the one with all the money in the bank. I checked Danny and Gurley; they're not quite so well off."

"If our Belarus friend, Bondar, is in this country, we need to find him."

"I'm trying."

"Thanks; this is great stuff. What else do you have?"

"There were many phone calls between Griffin and the guy who was killed in the hit-and-run, Larry Hoffman. At least twenty were in the month before Hoffman died."

"Could have easily been business," Laurie says. "Hoffman was in charge of providing some of Griffin's financing through Causeway."

"Unfortunately true. Or the same thing got both of them killed, by the same people."

"Any idea what that thing is?" she asks.

"No."

"Any idea who did it?"

"No."

She nods. "Now we're getting somewhere."

Sam has one more piece of news for us before he leaves, but it's not a positive. He's checked the towers to see which phones were at Jenny's house the night Griffin was killed. "Just Griffin's and Jenny's," he says. "No others in the area."

That's extremely unfortunate news . . . actually devastating. I was hoping that if another phone was there that I'd be able to point to the owner of that phone as a potential killer.

That idea is now out the window.

At this stage of a case, I approach everything with two things in mind.

One of them is obvious; I want to know what really happened, how things went down in the real world. But the other aspect can be equally important; I have to think in terms of what I can tell the jury.

In a perfect world those things would overlap; I could tell the jury the truth, they would lap it up with a spoon, and we could go home happy. That still could be the case this time, but it's so far down the road that it's not even in sight.

We aren't close to learning the truth, and we have very little to tell a jury. That has to change, or Jenny is going to be far and away the most famous inmate in state prison.

I obviously don't know who the real killer is, but I suspect it involves money. Griffin had a lot of it, but he took a lot more from other people. They seem to have been investments, but whatever returns they got, whether in money or something else, might have been unsatisfactory.

But unless I can come up with something totally solid, that's the kind of thing that will go over jurors' heads; it just feels vague and disconnected from the world that they will know. I would need far more information, concrete stuff, that I could hit them with before they would buy in.

The other area of Griffin's life that could have exposed him to danger was his drug use. Juries understand that; they instinctively know that's a dangerous world, run by people very capable of murder.

The problem is that I don't think for a minute that Griffin's death had anything to do with drugs. For one thing, drug dealers have no incentive to hurt or kill their customers unless they don't pay for the product, and I don't see anything that would have prevented Griffin from paying.

First of all, he obviously had the money. Second, it's the nature of drug users that they don't want to cut off their supplier . . . it sort of defeats the purpose.

Other things argue against this having to do with drugs. People in that world don't commit a murder and then elaborately set up someone else. They don't take the time to put two place settings down with cake crumbs on them. They put a bullet in someone's head and leave his body in the park.

And the break-in of the bungalow also makes the drug connection unlikely. It's just not how they operate; it's not the way they would scare me. Way too subtle.

When Laurie and I get home, Linda Ivers is there helping Jenny with some business stuff, but getting ready to leave. I ask her to stay for a minute, since I want to ask the same question of both of them.

"Have either of you ever heard of a guy named Sergey Bondar?" Jenny is more likely to know the name, since she spent far more time with Griffin, but if Linda spent time around the set, it can't hurt to ask her as well.

I get blank stares and shakes of the head from both of them. I'm about to show them the security tape of the bungalow when Linda's cell phone rings.

"Sorry," Linda says, before answering. Once she does, she says, "She's right here," and hands the phone to Jenny, who quickly tells the person that she will call back.

"That was Ed Markle, the director. He just wanted to check in and see how I'm doing."

I show Linda and Jenny the tape at the bungalow, but they both say that the person does not look familiar, with the disclaimer that because of the quality of the tape and the fact that the guy was looking away from the camera, it's hard to be sure.

Linda leaves and I call Audrey Dodge. After our *hellos*, she asks, "Making any progress?"

"Moving right along," I say. "Are you still in New York?"

"Yes. The work unraveling the film is done, but something else has come up. To what do I owe this call?"

"A name has surfaced in connection with the case, and I want to know if you're familiar with the person."

"Hope I can help. Who is it?"

"Sergey Bondar?"

"Sergey Bondar? What kind of name is that?"

"So you've never heard of him?"

"Afraid not. Who is he?" she asks.

"Let's just call him a person of interest."

"That sounds interesting; I can ask around."

"No need. Thanks for your time."

"Sorry I couldn't be more help. How's Jenny?"

"Hanging in there."

"Please give her my best."

'm in the den going through case documents and getting ready to go to bed when Laurie comes in. "Marcus needs us right away," she says.

I'm not sure I've ever heard the words *Marcus needs us* before. I mean, I've heard those words individually, but never strung together in that order in a sentence.

"Marcus needs us?" I ask, repeating the words to make sure I heard them correctly.

"Yes."

"Did he say why?"

"No, but I have the address," she says.

"And he said I should come also?"

"He did. Let's go."

Laurie is already walking toward the door, so I follow her. I'm not sure where Jenny is, but it doesn't matter, she's past the age where she needs a babysitter.

As we're getting into the car, I ask the next obvious question: "Where are we going?"

"The Bronx," she says as she programs the GPS. "Tremont Avenue."

"Should we call Corey?" As an ex-cop and partner to Laurie and Marcus, Corey can also handle himself quite well in dangerous situations. And his ex-police dog Simon Garfunkel is not a canine you want to mess with if you're a bad guy.

"Marcus said he already called him," Laurie says.

"Did Marcus sound like he was in trouble?"

She looks at me as if I'm nuts. That's understandable; while I don't keep records of these things, that has to be in the top three of the dumbest questions I've ever asked.

"Marcus?" she says. "In trouble?"

Enough said.

I've run out of questions.

At this late hour the drive to the George Washington Bridge only takes twenty minutes, and it's another ten to get to the Tremont Avenue address that Marcus gave Laurie. The building looks like an old warehouse, with the windows boarded up, at least the ones that we can see from the street. I can't see any lights coming from the inside of the building.

There is nothing about the looks of this situation that I like. Zero.

"What do we do now?" I ask, after Laurie parks in front of the building. In situations like this I don't exactly take control.

"Marcus said to go in, so we go in."

We get out of the car and I see that a gun has appeared in Laurie's right hand. It makes me simultaneously feel more secure and more worried. She can handle that gun and any trouble that comes along, but the mere fact that she has taken it out indicates there could be danger ahead.

I can deal with the fear . . . I just have to keep silently repeating to myself, *It's Marcus Clark. It's Marcus Clark. It's Marcus Clark.*

Laurie only hesitates for a moment, then tries the front door. It's open, and she walks in. I follow, mainly because what the hell else am I going to do?

It turns out that the reason we didn't see lights in the building is that the windows are covered over from the inside, either with black tape or some kind of thin fabric. The inside is actually lit up from an overhead light bulb, though not particularly bright.

The scene itself is something I'm not likely to soon forget. Lying in the middle of the floor are three men. They are on their backs, with their hands all tied together above their heads. By that I mean that all six hands seem to be bound together by what might be zip ties.

Their bodies themselves are spread out at angles so that they are almost like spokes on a wheel. One of them has his eyes closed; I'm hoping he's alive. The other two are conscious and staring at us as we walk toward them.

There is a desk along the far wall. Sitting on the chair behind it is a fourth man, conscious but looking none too happy. Leaning against the desk, and no doubt the cause of everything we have seen, is Marcus Clark.

I don't remember this situation coming up on the law boards.

Laurie walks over to Marcus and they talk for a brief while; I can't hear what they're saying, but I'm not trying too hard. I can't take my eyes off the human spokes on the floor. It seems if I walk over and push one of their legs with my foot, they would revolve around like a Las Vegas wheel.

But I think I'll fight off the urge to try it.

Laurie comes over to me and talks softly. "The guy at the desk is in charge of this operation. His name is Paulie Rivers, and he supplied Ryan Griffin with drugs. On that table over there are the records, which Marcus confirmed includes Griffin's name. He photographed the relevant pages."

In the room behind that door is what Marcus called a very large supply of drugs, enough to put this group away for a very long time.

"We should call the police," I say.

"Already done. Corey has a contact in the Bronx."

I nod and walk over to Rivers, who doesn't really brighten at my approach. "Paulie, rough day at the office?"

He doesn't respond, which annoys me. Nothing pisses me off more than being ignored by a drug dealer in a Bronx warehouse when I'm just trying to be friendly.

"Tell me about Ryan Griffin," I say.

"I'm not talking to you."

Marcus, who was leaning against the desk, straightens up. Paulie takes immediate notice of that; I can see the flash of fear in his beady eyes. I don't know exactly what Marcus did before we got here, but it obviously left a lasting imprint.

"Tell me about Ryan Griffin," I say again.

"What about him?"

"How much did he owe you?"

"He didn't owe me anything. He paid in advance; he ran a goddamn tab."

Running a tab and paying in advance are opposite concepts, but I decide not to point this out. Paulie is under a bit of stress, so a mistake like that is understandable. "Was he a heavy user?"

Rivers smirked, maybe gaining in confidence. "He liked what he liked."

At that point there is a loud noise and cops come pouring into the room, guns drawn and yelling for us all to drop our weapons, an unnecessary request since none of us is holding one.

With the apparent cop leader is Corey Douglas. "These three on the floor and the one behind the desk are the four bad guys," Corey says. "Everybody else is fine. Andy Carpenter, this is Lieutenant Breyer."

"The drugs are in the back room and that book over there has all the evidence you'll need," I say.

"Okay." He walks through the door into what is supposed to

be the supply room. He comes out with a smile on his face. "You guys did good. Very good."

"We can talk about it in court when you testify," I say.

He glares at me. "What does that mean?"

I smile. "Everything has a price."

ndy, come in here! You should see this."

I had woken up early this morning to walk the dogs, and then went back to sleep. Last night was a bit stressful and it tired me out. But now Jenny's voice is telling me to come into the den.

I put on a robe. I've had this robe for probably twenty years without ever wearing it. I don't remember when I got it or why, since I hate robes. Maybe I borrowed it from Shaquille O'Neal, since it's way too long, and I step on it when I walk. But I've started wearing it since Jenny came to live with us.

Laurie and Jenny are both in the den when I get there. They're watching CNBC, and being interviewed on the set are Audrey Dodge and Arnold Chrisman, Ryan Griffin's ex-wife and former business partner. There's a third person in the group, and the name on the screen under him identifies him as James Richards. Jenny was right; I should see this.

The chyron across the bottom of the screen says *"Elite" new subscription-based streaming service.*

Audrey is for the moment doing the talking. "I was going to contribute content as an outside producer, but when Ryan passed away, Arnold called me and asked me to come onboard on a full-time basis. I'll be the chief content officer, and Arnold is president and will be responsible for all business affairs."

The CNBC anchor says to Chrisman, "So you're all business and Audrey is creative?"

Chrisman smiles. "That's pretty much it. I know my limitations."

The anchor turns to James Richards. "And you're in charge of the technical end of this? The cyber work? Seems like a big job."

He smiles. "I have a good group that has already started and we're fairly far along. We'll make it happen."

The anchor seems to consider this uninteresting territory, so he doesn't follow up. Instead he turns back to Chrisman. "How are you going to compete with the huge streaming services already dominant in the market?"

"We're not trying to compete with them," Chrisman says. "We're going to stay in our lane, create quality entertainment, and make a profit doing it. That was Ryan's dream, and we're going to make it happen."

Audrey chimes in. "Back in the eighties, movie studios started creating classic divisions. They produced and released high-quality films, called art films at the time, that were designed to appeal to more upscale tastes. That in itself then became more mainstream and before long they were turning a healthy profit.

"Everywhere we go, people tell us that they want more than the action and sci-fi blockbusters, that they want films that make them think, while still being entertaining. That's what we're going to be about. Our advertising slogan to potential subscribers is *Put your money where your taste is*."

"It will take substantial funding to make this happen," the anchor points out. "Where—"

Chrisman interrupts. "We are fortunate that a lot of people believe in us and our business plan."

"Where will you be based?" the anchor asks.

"We'll be bicoastal," Chrisman says. "We'll have offices in New York and Los Angeles. Both cities are creative and business centers, and we will have a major presence in both."

Audrey smiles. "I see a lot of frequent flier miles in our future."

The anchor's last question is when Elite will be in operation, and Chrisman fields it. "We've been making acquisitions right along, and Ryan's two most recent films are ready to go as well. So we'll be making announcements as we go along, but the service should be up and running in six weeks."

The interview ends and I say, "Well, that's what Audrey meant when she said she was staying in New York because *something came up*."

"It's a strange choice," Jenny says. "First of all, I didn't think she and Arnold had much of a relationship. But beyond that, she's never been an executive. She's produced individual movies, but this company is going to have to do a lot and do it fast."

"Chrisman said they're buying programming from other sources," Laurie says.

Jenny nods. "I'm sure they are and will keep doing it, but they'll have to do a lot of original stuff too. It's the way these streaming services succeed. That costs big money. And then there's the money to set up the service in the first place . . . all that technology. I don't know much about that, but it can't be cheap."

"So why do it?" I ask. "Why enter a highly competitive, high-risk business like that? Bigger companies are losing a lot of money at it. They're all hoping to be among the last ones standing when others drop out. If Chrisman's company has the money to make movies, why not just make them like they've been doing?"

"I can't answer that," Jenny says. "I might have expected it from Ryan; he was more of a dreamer type. But Arnold is a serious, bottom-line-oriented businessman. This doesn't seem like his style."

"What about Audrey?"

Jenny smiles. "Taking over like this is her way of giving Ryan the finger in heaven, or wherever he is."

At this point I don't much care where he is; my only goal is to convince the jury that Jenny did not kill him. With that in mind, I head to the den to think about whether this newly announced company has any impact on our case.

I don't come up with much. There is always the possibility that some bad people wanted this to happen, and that somehow they saw Ryan's continued presence on this planet as an impediment to it.

But I don't know why that would have been the case. Ryan was said to be the driving force behind it, and his own considerable wealth could only have helped in that regard.

Maybe his increased dependence on drugs was making him erratic and unreliable, and as such he was considered dangerous to this business venture. But killing him seems like a drastic way to remove him, and people who invest in movies are not usually the killer types. They certainly are not above stabbing people in the back, but they do it metaphorically.

There has to be a reason that Ryan was a threat to someone. We're not going to know who until we know why, and we're not going to know why until we know who.

Things are moving right along.

They have to be laundering money."

    I say these words to Robby Divine in a phone call, after giving him the obligatory three minutes to bemoan the fate of the Chicago Cubs franchise. And I preface them by telling him I'm talking about the venture announced yesterday, the streaming service arrogantly named *Elite*.

"Are you telling me, or asking me?"

"Let me rephrase it . . . could they be laundering money?"

"If it's dirty, of course," he says.

"Do you think it is?"

"I don't make accusations without facts. I'm not a lawyer. I have a higher ethical standard. No offense."

"None taken. But that's less helpful than I was hoping for," I say.

"Let me put it this way. They are going to need a fortune in outside money. There are very few start-ups that don't come to me for money, because I am very rich and I like start-ups. But they were the exception; I haven't heard a word from them."

"I assume I am supposed to find that interesting?"

He ignores the question and continues. "And to my knowledge, no one I talk to has heard from them either. And except for you, I only talk to very rich people. Of course, neither I nor anyone I know would give them a dime anyway."

"Why?"

He scoffs at me. "Because the numbers can't work. With what

it would cost to set it up, and then the money they would spend buying and creating content, it doesn't make sense. The future of that business is in consolidation . . . existing companies are going to start eating their competitors. The market can't support all of them. So a new one is going to come along and compete?"

"They're going for a different niche, people who want higher quality. Not going for the blockbusters."

He laughs. "Good luck with that. You know why blockbuster movies become blockbuster movies? Because they are what people want to see and spend their money on."

He continues. "But let's say the new company does work, despite the odds. How big a profit can they ultimately turn, after losses the first few years? You can do better with T-bills."

"Any guesses where the money is coming from?"

"The kind of money we're talking about, it has to be foreign. And this is not a run-of-the-mill oligarch or arms dealer. Do you have any idea how much money it takes to create content for a streaming service?"

"I've heard, yes."

"We're talking about numbers higher than the GNP of some third-world countries."

"But if money laundering is the goal, whoever is supplying the money wouldn't care if their investments turn a profit, would they?"

"To a degree, they probably do, but it's not the point of the venture. The point is to wash the money and turn it from dirty to respectable. If they can make some along the way, that's a plus. Or if they lose some, that's okay too. But that is a secondary consideration."

"By the way, does the name Sergey Bondar mean anything to you?"

"Goaltender for the Vancouver Canucks?"

"No."

"Then I never heard of him."

"Thanks, you've been very helpful," I say.

"Andy, I can't tell you how much that thrills me."

Click.

I feel pretty good about money laundering as a theory for what is going on. Robby Divine, while being careful to point out that he has no specific knowledge of this situation, as much as confirmed it.

There is huge money being put into a business that at best could turn a small profit, and it is a stretch to even foresee that. Neither Robbie nor his wealthy friends would consider such an investment, and Chrisman must have known that, which is why they were not approached. The reason they wouldn't make that investment is that their money isn't dirty.

I don't know the source of that money, even though I know that most of it is coming through shell companies based in foreign countries. For the purposes of our case, that doesn't really matter. If the money needs to be laundered, that's good enough for us.

What we also don't know, and which is crucial, is why Ryan Griffin's death was necessary to further the plot. He must have been instrumental in starting it, yet suddenly it became important to remove him.

Corey Douglas has been looking into a parallel case, the hit-and-run death of Larry Hoffman, the hedge fund executive involved in funneling investment money to Griffin's firm. If his death was related to Griffin's, and I suspect it was, then he was another person it was deemed necessary to remove.

It's possible, even likely, that whatever prompted Griffin's murder also applied to Hoffman. Corey has found someone that he thinks I should meet with, so we've set it up for tomorrow morning.

In the meantime, with nothing else to do, I take the dogs for a walk. I just walked them a couple of hours ago, so this one is more for me than for them. I find that it clears my head, and while some people may not understand this, I also like spending time with them.

For them the world is a simple place; the sights and smells are enough to satisfy, as long as some petting and an occasional biscuit is thrown in. I love all three of them, but I have to admit Tara is special.

Tara is my friend, one of the best friends I have ever had.

"Andy, can we talk for a minute?"

I turn around and see Linda Ivers trying to catch up with us. She has again been at the house visiting Jenny and assisting her with whatever she needs. The other day Linda even offered to help me with anything . . . typing, bringing in takeout food, whatever.

I had asked her, "Do you mind if I call you Edna?"

"Why?"

"I just want to be able to ask Edna for something and get a positive response."

She's a bit out of breath, and we stop to let her reach us.

"There's something I should tell you. Maybe I should have said it earlier, but it could be nothing, and . . ."

"What is it?"

"I didn't want Jenny to hear this, in case it's . . . well, you know . . ."

The preamble to this story is moving incredibly slowly; Linda seems to be the Sebastian of storytellers. "I don't know anything, Linda, until I hear what you have to say."

Now that she has caught up to us, we start walking, more slowly this time. Sebastian is fine with that; the slower we walk the better he likes it.

"Okay, sorry," she says. "I'm just a little nervous. I overheard a conversation; it was between Ryan and Audrey Dodge. Actually, it was more than a conversation; it was an argument."

"When was this?"

"I think it was the day before he died. Could have been two days before."

"What were they arguing about?"

"I couldn't really tell; they were in her office at the production headquarters. I was walking by in the hall, and when I heard them raising their voices, I stopped to listen. I know I shouldn't have; it was none of my business."

"What did you hear?"

"It seemed to be about some business thing, something about doing something online. Maybe it was that streaming service that they just started, but I'm not really sure about that. I didn't hear enough of that part. But it got really personal."

"How so?"

"She was yelling that it was disgusting what he was doing; that he should leave Jenny alone and focus on doing his job. She was using some pretty bad language. And he was laughing . . . like, laughing at her . . . and calling her pathetic. He said the best move he ever made in his life was dumping her."

"Is that all?"

She hesitates. "No."

"What else did they say, Linda?"

"She said that she could kill him and wouldn't think twice about it."

"How did he respond?"

"He just laughed. He just kept laughing."

couldn't reach him; I just couldn't break through the wall," Pam Sparaco says. "It was the most frustrating experience of my life."

Sparaco was Larry Hoffman's fiancée at the time he died in the hit-and-run on First Avenue in Manhattan. She is herself an attorney with a New York law firm, but was willing to meet me in New Jersey, because she was already going to be here visiting her parents.

We're having coffee in an Englewood diner on Route 9, and I can hear the emotion in her voice as she talks. "He was always this fun guy; everybody liked him, and he would do anything for his friends."

"When were you going to be married?" I ask.

"We weren't."

"I thought you were engaged. Doesn't the marriage part come after that?"

"We were engaged, but I was going to break it off."

"Mind if I ask why?"

"Larry had become so distant, so disconnected from me, that I just couldn't justify moving forward. If that was what it was like before we got married . . . well, it wasn't going to work."

"So you hadn't told him yet?"

"No, and I'm glad I didn't actually do it, because then I might blame myself even more."

"You blame yourself for his death?"

"In a way. Something was bothering Larry; no, that's not strong enough. It was torturing him. If I had been able to get him to open up, I might have helped him deal with it."

"But you don't know what it was?"

"No, he wouldn't tell me. He denied that there was anything to tell. But it had to have something to do with his work."

"Could he have been worried about money?"

"No chance. He was doing great financially, especially the last couple of years. We were going on amazing vacations, all first class. And he bought an apartment that cost almost four million dollars."

"Any chance one of those vacations you went on was to the Caymans?"

She looks surprised. "How did you know that?"

"Lucky guess. Did he do any business while you were there?" I don't bother pointing out that a Caymanian business invested in Griffin's company, or that Sam had discovered Bondar was there three times.

She nods. "Yes . . . I stayed on the beach and read one day while he went to some meetings. I remember at the time I didn't think they went well, because he seemed preoccupied and worried. I asked him, but he said everything was fine, and he seemed okay for the rest of the trip. That is, if okay includes being paranoid."

"How was he paranoid?"

"In a lot of ways. He was always concerned that we, or he, was being watched. I remember one time on that Caymans trip, we were at dinner, and he was staring across the room. He looked away, but asked me to look in that direction and tell me if a guy at the bar was looking at us."

"Was he?"

"Not that I could tell. He was just sitting there drinking."

"Anything else?"

"One time I wanted to use his computer to order something online, but he kept watching over my shoulder to make sure I didn't click on anything I wasn't supposed to. He was totally freaked out about it; he was afraid of viruses or something, I guess. I was worried about him; I thought maybe he should go on some kind of meds."

What she has just said has given me an idea. "Any chance I could get a look at his computer? There might be clues to what happened in there."

She thinks about it for a few moments and says, "I'll get it to you."

"You have it?"

She nods, a bit sadly. "I have everything. He left it all to me. He had no family, I was his fiancée, and he had no idea I was planning to end it." Then, "A pretty sad way to become rich."

"Don't beat yourself up over it; you did nothing wrong."

"Thank you."

"Can I have someone pick up the computer from you?"

"Sure." She tells me to have someone come by her office tomorrow, and my plan is to ask Sam to do it, since he'll be the one analyzing it anyway.

"Did Larry ever talk about Ryan Griffin?" I ask.

"Of course. Ryan was his boss for a while, and then when he went to California, they were still connected in some way. We had dinner with Ryan and Audrey Dodge quite a few times."

"In the last few months before he died, did he ever say anything to you about Ryan that seemed unusual?"

She thinks for a few moments. "No, not really. I know they were still talking a lot, but that was normal. They did business together, and they were friends."

I'm out of questions, so I thank her for talking to me.

"Mr. Carpenter . . ."

"Andy."

"Andy, all these questions . . . do you think Larry was targeted? That the hit-and-run driver singled him out?"

I see no reason to lie to her. "I do, but at this point I don't know why."

"I do as well," she says.

"Why?"

"I guess it's sort of like that old saying, *Just because you're paranoid doesn't mean someone isn't really after you.*"

I didn't learn anything really concrete from my conversation with Pam Sparaco, certainly nothing I can use in court. But it did reaffirm my feeling that there was something going on with Griffin's business that threatened some very dangerous people, who acted to remove the threat.

As I'm heading home, Sam calls me on my cell. "I found Bondar, or at least his phone."

"Terrific."

"But in the process, I found out something else."

"What's that?" I ask.

"Can you meet me at the office? I need to show it to you."

"Is it important?"

"Very."

"Should I have Laurie meet us there?" I ask.

"Good idea. And maybe Marcus and Corey."

We're assembled in my office about forty-five minutes after I got off the phone with Sam.

Laurie is here, but I opted not to bring in Marcus and Corey. I want to judge the importance of what Sam has to say first; he has a tendency toward the dramatic. We can always update Marcus and Corey as needed when we find out what the hell is going on.

"As I mentioned, Bondar's phone originated in Belarus," Sam says. "I was able to penetrate the phone company's computer there, but it didn't do me any good. Their equipment is not sophisticated enough; not only couldn't I find the location of the phone that way, but they wouldn't be able to either, if they tried."

"But you found it anyway," Laurie says.

Sam nods. "Yes, but I had to do it through the towers. That makes it hit or miss, usually miss. Under ordinary circumstances, I would have to be extremely lucky to find it that way. Fortunately, or maybe unfortunately, these were extraordinary circumstances."

Sam lays out some maps and computer charts on my desk. I don't understand them, and I don't want to learn. I just want to hear whatever the hell Sam is talking about.

He points to one chart and says, "I found Bondar's phone for the first time right here. And the reason I did was that I was also monitoring the phones for the three guys at Master Security, Ruben, Danny, and Gurley. Bondar was at the Fordham Road location with them."

"When?"

"At the same time you were."

This is something of a stunner. "We didn't see him there." I turn to Laurie, and she nods. She's as confused by this as I am.

"This is not an exact science," Sam says. "Although it's close. Bondar wasn't necessarily in the building with you. He could have been outside, but I'd bet it was less than fifty yards away."

"So he would have seen us go in and out," I say. "Maybe he was there because he was following us."

"That can't be," Sam says. "He got there first. I checked your phone records. I hope you don't mind."

Neither Laurie nor I mind, so Sam continues. "From that point on, I watched to see if Bondar's phone intersected with the security guys again, and they did last week."

"At their office," I ask.

"No, in Suffern, New York. According to Google Maps, it's some kind of abandoned park, or vacant lot. Ruben, Gurley, and Bondar all had their phones there. Danny did not."

"How long were they there?" Laurie asks.

"That's the interesting part. Now I'm only talking about the location of their phones, you know? I'm not saying anything about where they were, just their phones."

"Understood," I say.

"Well, based on that, if their phones remained with them, then Ruben and Gurley don't seem to have left. Their phones went dark that night and have not been on the grid since."

"What about Bondar's phone?" I ask.

"He left there with it. I found him again this morning when I was going over the data. I know where he was last night."

"Where?" Laurie asks.

"Your house."

"What?" I ask, reflexively, though I know I heard him correctly. "He was at our house?"

Sam nods. "Again, I don't necessarily mean in the house itself, but he was very close. There's no doubt about it."

Now I know why Sam suggested that Marcus and Corey come to this meeting. I need to give Sam more credit.

"So I just want to understand something about how this phone situation works . . . how the Belarus thing complicates it. You can't automatically know where the phone is? You can't follow it? But you can watch specific locations, and if it turns up there, you will know it?"

"Correct. That's the best I can do."

"So if we wanted to know when he came near our house again, you could tell us?"

"I should be able to, yes. I wish I could be more certain, but this is an unusual situation."

"If we went about this legally, with subpoenas, could we get better information?" Laurie asks.

Sam shakes his head. "No. You could own the Belarus phone company, and you still couldn't get them to provide it. They don't have the capability."

"It wouldn't matter anyway," I say. "Attempting to serve a subpoena on a company there would be a waste of time. Even getting one here would take too long. Having said that, I am going to ask Eddie Dowd to get legal subpoenas for all the phone records that Sam has already accessed. That way we can use it in court if we want to."

"Good idea," Laurie says. Then, "So now what? How do we deal with what Sam has just told us?"

"I don't know yet. But we need to come up with a way to play it all to our advantage," I say. "And our client's."

There is a great deal to digest in what Sam has uncovered.

For one thing, we've learned that an international fugitive killer was watching our house. I feel confident that he's not looking to make an offer on it; international fugitive killers would want to live in a more cosmopolitan city than Paterson.

Laurie has just gotten off the phone with Cindy Spodek, our friend who is fairly high up in the FBI. She had asked Cindy for any information the Bureau has on Bondar, and Cindy just called her back.

I've convened a meeting in the house with Laurie, Marcus, Corey, and myself. Corey has brought along his former police dog and partner, Simon Garfunkel. Simon's presence brings the total number of non-cowards in the room to four.

I'm sure Jenny senses that something is going on, but I did not invite her to sit in. I'm going to have to tell her some of this; she has a right to know that a dangerous person has been watching the house that she's living in. But I don't want to share with her, or anyone, what our plan will be, should we come up with one.

Actually, Jenny's presence in the house is the reason we are meeting here and not my office. We have to assume that she is in some danger; she might even be the target, for a reason we are not yet aware of. We are not going to leave her alone.

I start the meeting by saying, "Whatever we do about this

situation, we first need to weigh the effect it will have on our client and our case. That has to be our first priority, along with the personal safety of the lead attorney on the case. Now, why do we think Bondar was watching this house?"

"I see three possibilities," Laurie says. "In no particular order . . . one, he was casing the house, looking for the best way to make an entry when the time was right for him to do so. Two, he was monitoring our movements and patterns, when we go in and out, when you walk the dogs, et cetera. And three, he was trying to learn if Jenny was actually staying here; that has not been reported in the press."

"What does he gain from any of that?" I ask.

"If we're right, then Bondar is in the threat removal business. He eliminated Larry Hoffman, Ryan Griffin, and possibly the three security goons," Corey says. "He must see one of us, probably you, as a potential threat and therefore a possible target."

"Which means he must think you know something about whatever the conspiracy is," Laurie says.

"I wish he was right about that," I say.

"Maybe he is, at least partially. We are not in the total dark here," Laurie says. "We have good reason to believe that this is about laundering money."

"That's our belief, but we can't come close to proving it. They have insulated themselves very well with their shell companies in various countries. It doesn't seem like a good enough reason for them to go around murdering people."

"What did Cindy have to say about Bondar?" I ask.

"Quite a bit. First of all, he is extremely dangerous, a cold-blooded killer who has mastered his craft. He is generally in the employ of a billionaire Russian oligarch named Yaroslav Miranov."

"Let me guess . . . Miranov is on occasion engaged in criminal activities."

"Very much so," Laurie says. "Pretty much anything you can think of—arms dealing, drug smuggling, cybercrimes. His people are considered responsible for that cyberattack on the French power grid, where they received a large ransom for putting it back online. Of course, Miranov denies all of it. But Cindy has no doubt that he is involved in money laundering."

"Big money," Corey says.

Laurie nods. "Very big. But not big enough. When I told Cindy how much these streaming services spend, she said even Miranov wouldn't be able to handle it. But whatever he was doing, Bondar would enforce it. She must have said *be careful* ten times in our call."

"This is depressing," I say. "Let's get back to what Sam had to say about Bondar and the security guards."

"Maybe Bondar thinks they told us something, if he was watching when we were there," Laurie says.

Corey says, "It seems to be a reasonable assumption that they were either murdered, or have been kidnapped. We have an obligation to deal with that one way or the other."

I nod. "I agree, and I have an obligation as defense counsel to try and use that situation to our advantage."

"What does that mean?" Corey asks, challenging. As an ex-cop, he is not always sympathetic to the tactics that we defense attorneys employ. It's a struggle for him, and I understand that, but I cannot let it influence me.

"One way or another, we are going to have to bring Bondar into our trial. He is a killer, he had contact with Griffin, and he is someone we can point to and tell the jury that they have to consider the possibility that Bondar, and not Jenny, put the knife in Griffin's back. He is our key to reasonable doubt, and at this point the only one we have."

I continue, "Whatever might have happened to those three guys, if we can identify Bondar as the perpetrator, it would be a huge boost to our case. We cannot prove that Jenny did not commit the murder, so we have to be able to say that someone else might have. Bondar is the perfect candidate to play the role of *someone else*."

"But Bondar is not behind all this. Based on what we know about him, he's a hired gun. He must have bosses like Miranov calling the shots," Laurie says.

"True. But our goal here is to implicate a potential killer. We can't give the jury an accountant, or a CFO brandishing a spreadsheet, or even a billionaire oligarch. Our client is on trial for murder, not fraud."

"So one way or another, we have to get Bondar," Laurie says.

I nod. "We do, and hopefully before he gets us." Then, "So how do we do that? The floor is open for suggestions."

Corey says, "The first thing is getting out to that park in Suffern to try and figure out what happened. Andy, Simon, and I can do that."

"That could be dangerous," Laurie says. "I'll go with you."

"Sam can make sure that Bondar is not there when we go," I say.

Laurie shakes her head. "He can only make sure that his phone isn't there. And we don't know who else might be there, or who might be involved. We can't be positive what we'd be walking into."

"There's more danger here," I point out. "This house seems to be Bondar's potential next move."

"Marcus can stay here in case Bondar shows up," Laurie says. "Marcus, are you okay with that?"

Marcus, who hasn't said a single word the entire meeting, keeps his record intact and just nods.

That says it all.

W e don't drive into the park area in Suffern.

Even though Sam has confirmed that Bondar, or at least his phone, is not on the scene, we are being very careful. So we park a few hundred yards away, and Corey and Simon walk ahead to scout out the situation. If there is anyone there, Simon will literally sniff it out well before we would.

It's about ten long minutes before Corey and Simon come back into view and Corey is waving us ahead. Apparently the coast is clear.

They turn and walk back toward the area in question as Laurie and I follow. The road is dusty; it has been very hot and hasn't rained in a couple of weeks, which may work in our favor as we look for clues as to what happened here.

Corey and Simon are walking around, looking at the ground, and Corey signals us to come over to where they are. They're standing near a rusted swing set with chains coming down from the top bar, but no actual seats.

"This area has been raked over," Corey says. "Get a picture of it."

Laurie takes out her cell phone and snaps a few shots. Corey then picks up a branch and moves some of the dirt. There are some stains that look very much like blood, though I have to admit I am not an expert on blood-stained dirt.

Corey doesn't say anything; he doesn't have to. Laurie takes pictures of the stains. Simon, for his part, seems excited about something, but he won't leave Corey's side, even though he is not on a leash.

"Show us, Simon," Corey says, and Simon is off in a flash. He runs to an area just inside the tree line, and we follow along. Simon is amazingly fast; even at nine years old he can really move. He covers the distance in seconds; it would take Sebastian five minutes, and he'd want to stop and nap along the way.

As we follow, Laurie points to the ground. "Something has been dragged here. Something or someone."

Simon has stopped and is barking. He's in a small clearing behind the first grouping of trees. We reach him and Corey puts his hand on Simon's head to calm him down. The effect is immediate.

There is an area that Simon is interested in; it has some branches and brush on it, but it's in the open. There is no reason that the material should be there and placed in the way it is. It was obviously put there intentionally, probably to conceal what is underneath.

Laurie takes photos of all of this, and Corey moves some of the branches on one end. He signals to Laurie to come over and get some more photos.

"These are graves," Corey says. "I'm sure of it, and Simon is even more sure."

"Doesn't look like Bondar took that much effort to conceal them," I say.

Corey nods. "True, but this is not exactly a highly traveled area, and bad weather would have camouflaged it more. But I don't think Bondar cared much one way or the other if the graves were eventually found."

"This is one cold-blooded son of a bitch we're dealing with," Laurie says.

There's nothing more to be learned here, at least not by us. Forensics could probably have a field day at this site, and one way or another we are going to have to get them out here. And it would be best to do it soon, before it rains and washes away much of the evidence.

We head back to the house, discussing the situation along the way. Simon, who has done more than his part, opts not to be included in the conversation; he is content to lie on the back seat, munching on a chewy.

"As much as I hate the concept, we have to draw Bondar out," I say.

"Why do you say that?" Laurie asks, although I suspect she knows.

"For a few reasons. Right now, he controls the terms and the timing. He can come at us, come at me, whenever he chooses. We are playing defense, and that is never preferable. For another, we want to get the cops up to the site in Suffern as soon as we can. And lastly, the trial is almost upon us, and Bondar is the key."

"You recognize the danger?" Corey asks.

I laugh; I can't help it. "Do I recognize the danger? Is there a person in the galaxy who dislikes danger more than me? My danger detector is a finely tuned instrument."

Corey smiles. "I wasn't talking about the danger to you; that exists whether we draw him out on our terms or not. I was talking about Bondar having the opposite reaction if we try and provoke him. He could go underground and we'd never find him until it's way too late."

"It's a possibility," I say. "But that's not how I think it would play out. Whatever they are trying to cover up, whether it's the money laundering or something else, that's their priority. Bondar is just the instrument; if he has to disappear after doing his job, he'll disappear. He'll go back to Belarus and get a talk show."

"I agree with Andy, for a number of reasons, the biggest one selfish," Laurie says. "Ricky's coming home next week; I don't want us sitting in that house wondering if Bondar is going to come at us. One way or another we need to take him out before then."

Corey nods. "Fair enough. But we still need to figure out the best way to do it."

"Vince is about to become one happy camper," I say.

There are a few reasons why I've decided to give Vince the interview.

For one thing, it doesn't matter who I give it to. The media attention on this is such that I could give it to the Paterson Penny-Saver and it would take off like wildfire. For another, Vince is a friend, and this exclusive will be a huge feather in his cap.

But most important, I'm giving it to Vince because I will be able to control the message, and I trust him. He wouldn't break our agreed-upon ground rules, because he is an outstanding journalist, and a good friend, and I would never buy him another meal at Charlie's if he did.

I call Vince and ask him to come to my office. He complains, because that is his nature. He would complain if I called to tell him he won the lottery.

"That shithole," he says, referring to my office. "Can't we meet someplace nicer? Like the city dump?"

"Vince, I am about to give you a story that *60 Minutes* would jump at," I say, exaggerating only slightly. "If you're not here in thirty minutes, you will not be admitted to this dump."

"It's important?"

"It's important," I say.

Part of our definition of friendship is that when something is labeled important, no more questions are asked. Vince will be here, whether it is something that benefits him or benefits me. Important is important.

Vince arrives in nineteen minutes, and he comes up the steps with a peach in his hand from Sofia's fruit stand downstairs. I don't know if he paid for it or swiped it, and I don't want to know.

"This better be good," he says.

"You can be the judge of that, and if it doesn't meet your high journalistic standards, you can pass on the opportunity. But first we have to establish some ground rules."

"Uh-oh."

"I am going to be telling you the defense strategy in the Jenny Nichols case. You cannot quote me; you can only attribute the story to *a source close to the defense*. The judge will still know it's me and will strangle me, but I still can't be directly quoted."

"No problem. Is that it?"

"Not quite. I'm going to tell you some things to give you a complete picture, but you can only include in the story the stuff that I say is on the record. The rest you will have to take to your grave, which will be sooner than you think, if you screw this up."

"Okay."

"And as you know as well as I do, this case is so huge that you are going to be hounded once your story breaks. Every news network is going to want your ugly face in their studio to do interviews. No matter what they ask you, you cannot go further than what is in the original story."

"Got it. I hope this story isn't time sensitive because it is taking you forever to tell it to me."

So I do tell it to him. Not nearly all of it, and certainly no information on conversations I have had with my client. But I tell him all about Bondar, without getting into the underlying money-laundering claims. I tell him that there were business reasons that Griffin was killed, and I talk about the security guys that are missing.

I say that they were last seen in Suffern, New York, and that I expect to have more information on it soon. I don't mention the Larry Hoffman connection because I want to save something special just for the jury.

I also give Vince an Interpol photograph of Bondar and he quotes my request asking that any sightings of Bondar be reported to a tip line we are setting up. It's the only time I let him quote me.

Obviously in doing all this I recognize the possibility that it will have the opposite effect to what we are hoping for. Corey was right; he could go underground and either hide or leave the country. The bet I'm making, and it's a risky one, is that it will not deter him, and in fact speed him up.

Of course, that carries its own significant risk. Speeding up someone who is trying to kill me may not be the smartest move.

Another important fact is that through Vince I am also sending a message to the potential jurors, all of whom will either read or hear about this development. The story is so dominant in the media, and has been for so long, that no one can miss it.

The judge is going to be pissed.

And so is Bondar.

I'm more afraid of Bondar, and it's not close.

wish my predictions could be this accurate when I'm betting on football games.

I'd be so rich I'd never have to work again. Actually, I'm already so rich that I never have to work again, but I seem to keep on working. The only thing I'm worse at than gambling is retirement.

But this time I correctly predicted two out of two, right on the head.

The truth is, they were easy predictions to make. For one thing, I knew that the media world would go nuts over Vince's story. The public has been starving for new developments in Jenny's case, and Vince served up a large helping.

It is the lead story on every newscast, and CNN has just promoted the fact that Vince Sanders will be on live in the next segment. He's probably spent the last two hours combing what little hair he has.

The other sure-thing prediction I made was that Judge Slater would take a dim view of the article. At 8 A.M. I got a call that the judge wanted to see me and James Shaffer in her chambers at 9 A.M.

I was going to complain about the short notice, but my self-preservation instinct kicked in and I thought better of it. So I'm at the courthouse now, and when I head back to the judge's chambers, I see that Shaffer is already out in the corridor, waiting for me so we can enter together.

"Did you wear your bulletproof vest?" he asks, smiling. He's going to enjoy this. The reason I know this is that if the roles were reversed, I'd be savoring every minute.

"Sometimes you have to take one for the team," I say.

We are led into the judge's chambers. She sits behind her desk, her face set into a look meant to convey her extreme displeasure. It's a look that every judge I know has mastered.

"So, like every other person on planet Earth, I woke up this morning bombarded with the defense's strategy in the case," Judge Slater says. "My first reaction was, this couldn't be, because I had explicitly warned against this happening in a bench conference. Can anyone explain?"

"I'm afraid I cannot, Your Honor," Shaffer says, loving the situation.

I've decided to tackle this head on. "I can, Your Honor. I spoke to the reporter."

"Exactly why did you do that?" she asks, while trying to decide my method of execution.

"For two reasons. First, I felt that to properly represent my client, I needed to even the playing field."

"Explain," she says.

"When this case began, Mr. Shaffer held a press conference to announce the charges against my client. He took questions, and it went on for almost twenty-five minutes."

"That was standard practice in a case of this kind, Your Honor," Shaffer says.

I shake my head. "I'm not sure what you mean by *a case of this kind*. Your Honor, I took the liberty of examining your docket this year. You presided over two other murder trials. In neither case did the prosecution hold a press conference to announce the charges against the accused."

Shaffer starts to say something, but I continue. "The reason that it was done here is because of the media attention, I understand that. But that same media attention is why you cautioned us against going to the press. Mr. Shaffer did it once, that I know of, and now I have evened the playing field."

"And your other reason?"

"It is vital to our case that we locate Sergey Bondar. We are not a law enforcement agency, and we do not have Mr. Shaffer's vast resources at our disposal. And Bondar is a man used to evading detection; his name has been laminated on Interpol's most-wanted list. Asking the public for help is the only option we have."

The judge turns to Shaffer, who is ready with a reply. "Your Honor, the defense has pulled an international fugitive out of thin air in a desperate attempt to influence the potential jurors out there. It would be akin to us telling the press that Ms. Nichols was seen with Al Capone.

"Mr. Carpenter is well aware that news like this will be lapped up by the media with a spoon, and he now has the jury pool thinking that this Bondar character just might be the guilty party. All of this without any evidence whatsoever."

"If we have no evidence, Your Honor, your instructions to the jury will seal our fate," I say. "But that is not how this will play out. I can promise you that."

She frowns. "And I can promise both of you, and especially you, Mr. Carpenter, that if there is another episode like the one this morning, I will hold you in contempt of this court, and the sanctions will be varied and considerable."

"I understand, Your Honor."

"Good day, gentlemen."

We leave the chambers. Since I am not in handcuffs, I would have to say that the meeting went well.

As I leave the courthouse, the media is out in force, bombarding me with questions. I avoid every one with a simple "No comment."

The judge would be proud of me.

This is a rather unusual jury selection, I think unlike any I have participated in.

Usually the overwhelming majority of potential jurors would rather sit in a dentist's chair than the jury box. They come armed with excuses and with answers that they hope will disqualify them.

Of course, that is not true of everyone. Some of them are bored with their everyday existence, and see a jury trial as comparatively interesting. Or some see it as a way out of work, usually with pay.

I've heard there are also some people who see serving on a jury as their civic duty, and want to do their part to help our system function and see justice prevail. Like I say, I've heard that those people exist; they are the stuff of legend. But I haven't actually run into any of them.

They are the Sasquatches of the legal world.

But this case turns all that on its head. Because of Jenny's celebrity, and because of the intense media interest, getting on the jury is better than winning a ticket to the Super Bowl.

It's a brush with fame, and a story that a person can tell for the rest of his or her life. It's even better than the *I dated Jenny Nichols in high school* story that I have gotten such great mileage out of.

I would imagine that more than half of the potential jurors

see a book deal in their future, since everybody knows that any dope can write a book.

So instead of trying to get out of serving, these people will want to get in. They will try to say things that we want to hear. But it's tricky, because they know they have to be palatable to both sides.

So they have to play it down the middle and sound thoughtful and impartial. That way both sides will hate them, and accept them as jurors.

Getting Jenny in and out of the courtroom requires D-Day–type planning. Despite the fact that four million photographs of Jenny exist in the world, the goal is to get the next one, the one of her arriving to face her accusers. For the moment, at least, it is the Holy Grail of photographs.

Judge Slater won't let her travel with me, so bailiffs arrive at our house every morning to pick her up, and then they take her back after court ends for the day. They're not thrilled to have to wait each time while she says goodbye to Mamie.

We have successfully snuck her in for the second day in a row now, and I think it's fair to say that every person in the packed gallery has not taken their eyes off of her. I've instructed her to look interested but not emotional, and she has managed that easily.

The jury we have finally seated has seven women and five men, five African Americans and two Hispanic men. There was speculation in the press that because Jenny is so attractive, it would be better to get men on the jury. Women, they felt, might be threatened and jealous.

Others opined that women would better understand what might have driven Jenny to plunge a knife into an abusive boyfriend, even though that is not Jenny's defense. Men, those people feel, would be less understanding.

So based on that, I would say we should have gone for neither men nor women.

I'm fine with the jury that we picked, or maybe I'm not. I won't really know until I know, and I'll find out at the exact moment it will be too late to do anything about it.

During the voir dire process, Judge Slater alerted everyone to the very real possibility that she would choose to sequester them for the duration of the trial, which she estimated could be as long as two weeks. She wanted them to speak up if sequestering would impose any intolerable hardships on them. Nobody did.

Once the panel was seated, she dropped the bomb on them. Because of the intense media coverage, which Judge Slater had said might be too overwhelming to avoid, she was, in fact, sequestering them.

It was probably the right decision, especially since most of the jurors would likely not have followed her directive to avoid reading or hearing about the case. This way they have no choice.

Tonight I'll prepare for opening statements, but not too heavily. My approach is to know the points I want to cover, but to be unscripted and spontaneous. I also want to be able to react to whatever Shaffer has to say in his opening.

Basically I know what he will say, that Jenny is a killer and should go to prison for the rest of her life.

My plan is to disagree.

Lawyers weren't built to withstand this kind of pressure, at least not lawyers named Andy Carpenter.

We are designed to have meetings, and conference calls, and long lunches sipping wine and telling stories about difficult judges we've dealt with, about law school buddies who were disbarred and went to prison for fraud.

In extreme, rare situations, we are prepared to deal with the rigors of a trial, the intense preparation necessary, and the often extremely high stakes. Lives and fortunes can turn on the decisions that juries render, and it is up to lawyers to influence and guide them in making those decisions.

I have all that weighing on me in this case, and the pressure is heightened by the remarkable level of media coverage. People are watching for news of this trial all over the world; they are probably opening the show with it every morning on *Good Morning Yemen*.

But of course, that's not nearly all of it. Hovering over everything is the knowledge that an international killer is after me; we are just waiting for him to make a move. It's been three days since we tried to goad him into action with Vince's newspaper story, but apparently Bondar doesn't respond quickly to goading.

We're all set up and ready. Either Marcus or Corey is watching me at all times, and when I'm home they are monitoring the house. Laurie is obviously there as well; in this case the little woman protects the husband, not the reverse. We're enlightened that way.

Sam is monitoring the cell towers to determine when Bondar is in our neighborhood. He cautions us that it is an inexact science, but he's hopeful that he can give us adequate warning. That would be nice.

The difficulty in waiting is intensified by the fact that Ricky will be home in three days. If we don't have a resolution by then, we are going to have to figure out a plan. He simply cannot be in the house with the specter of Bondar hovering over us.

We've tried to behave normally, so as not to scare Bondar off, although the idea of scaring him off has considerable appeal to me. I'm even walking the dogs on a regular basis, though the walks are far shorter than usual, and I know that I am being watched by our team at all times.

Even so, it's nerve-wracking.

It's entirely possible that the publicity had the reverse effect, something we had realized was a risk. Bondar could have gone underground to escape detection, or even left the country, especially since Sam has for the time being lost track of his phone. If that turns out to be the case, we will have to go to plan B, after we come up with a plan B.

This afternoon I alerted Pete Stanton to the possibility of bodies buried in the Suffern park. As a captain in the Paterson Police Department, he obviously has no jurisdiction there, but he conducted a joint operation with the Suffern police and they discovered the graves.

Naturally, Pete asked me how I knew about the scene in Suffern, and I lied and said I had gotten an anonymous tip as a result of Vince's article. He knows that my explanation was horseshit, and he knows that I know he knows, but he'll accept it and move on. I wasn't about to tell him that Sam illegally hacked the phone company.

Tonight I am again going through documents readying myself for my opening statement, and for Shaffer's early witnesses. I'm already prepared, but there can always be something that I've missed.

The NFL preseason is in full swing, so I'll have a game on as background noise as I work. I'm a confirmed football maniac, but even I find the preseason insufferably boring. It doesn't even make for good background noise.

Mamie comes into the room and jumps up on my lap. She is a glutton; she will go anywhere for petting at any time. Since she has been here she has gotten more petting per pound than any dog in America.

At ten fifteen the phone rings; the sound is jarringly loud in the house. I'm hoping it's a wrong number, or a telemarketer, but my gut knows better.

It's showtime.

Laurie answers it and the conversation lasts less than ten seconds. When she gets off, she simply says, "Marcus has him. Let's go." I see Laurie is already holding her handgun; she also believes in being prepared.

"Where are we going?" I ask, but she is already on the move toward the back of the house. She either didn't hear the question or is ignoring it. When danger looms, I seem to become invisible.

Jenny comes out of her room, having heard the commotion. "What's going on?"

"Stay here," I say. "We'll be back."

I follow Laurie out the back door into the backyard. Our outside lights are set to go on from movement, which is why they are now lit up.

A man that I have to assume is Bondar is standing facing the wall, his arms against it and his legs spread. Marcus stands less than a foot behind him, holding a handgun on him.

"Was he armed, Marcus?"

Marcus nods and points toward the garage. Laurie walks over to pick up Bondar's gun, where Marcus must have thrown it.

"Bondar, where've you been?" I ask. "We've been waiting for you."

He doesn't say anything, so I ask Marcus. "Can you turn him around?"

Marcus grabs Bondar by the arm and turns him so that he is facing me. If looks could kill, Vince would be publishing my obituary in tomorrow's paper. He's told me that it has been written for years, and that he enjoys periodically updating it.

I am struck by the size disparity between the two men. Bondar is enormous; if you saw him and Marcus on a football field, you would take him for a lineman and Marcus for a defensive back.

I ask Bondar a number of questions, mostly trying to get him to talk about the conspiracy; whether he killed Griffin, Hoffman, and the security guys; and what the hell is going on.

He doesn't react in any way, just continues sneering, but then suddenly spits at Marcus.

He spit at Marcus Clark. As stupid maneuvers go, that ranks well above tugging on Superman's cape and pulling the mask off that old Lone Ranger.

I don't know if it lands on Marcus or not; I can't see in the dim light. Marcus doesn't recoil or wipe anything off.

All he does is toss his gun aside.

I have seen him do this before.

Bondar accepts the challenge. He may realize that Laurie is standing nearby with two guns at the ready, hers and Bondar's. But it doesn't matter; right now it's just the two men, Bondar and Marcus. And one of them is really stupid.

Bondar throws the first punch, but Marcus slips it and moves inside. He punches Bondar in the gut, and it lands with a thud, stunning the larger man. His reaction is to grab Marcus and try to envelop him in a bear hug. It's a smart move, considering his size advantage.

Marcus pushes him and simultaneously pulls away, but as he does so he launches an uppercut kick to Bondar's groin. To continue the football analogy from before, if a placekicker used that much force on a field goal attempt, it would be good from sixty yards.

Bondar lets out the most horrible scream I have ever heard; it resounds so loudly that our neighbors must be taking cover under their beds. It does not last long, though, as Marcus clubs him across the side of the head with his elbow, and he immediately goes silent. Unconsciousness will do that to you.

Laurie tells me to call the police, but as I go to do so, I see Pete Stanton pull up along with four squad cars. Marcus had called Corey, who in turn called Pete.

"There's the guy Vince wrote about," I say, pointing at Bondar, out cold on the ground. "He's responsible for the deaths in Suffern, and a lot more."

"Is he alive?" Pete asks.

I shrug. "Whatever."

My phone rings, and it's Sam. "Bondar is at your house, Andy," he says, urgency in his voice. "I picked up his phone on the grid."

"He's right here. We're having a couple of beers and watching the Mets game," I say. "You want to talk to him?"

"What the hell does that mean? I'm serious."

"I know, Sam. Thanks. Everything's under control."

I hang up and leave Laurie to answer any further questions Pete may have, while I go inside to tell my client about a new development in her case.

Then I am going to call Vince and give him another story.

The good news is that Vince's version of what happened last night has created another media firestorm.

And this is not one the judge can blame me for; it is something that happened and was reported on. The police were involved; I haven't created or orchestrated anything.

Well, actually I have, but it's nothing she could know about or use against me.

In fact, she was sympathetic and solicitous; she called Shaffer and me into her chambers before the start of court and inquired as to my well-being. We all agreed that this was nothing that should delay the trial from starting.

The bad news, and it is considerable, is that the jury will not know any of this, at least not now. They are sequestered and shielded from all news about the trial. I will definitely try to inform them about it through witness testimony, but it will depend on the judge admitting it. And it definitely will not have the same impact as the media explosion everyone else is experiencing.

Shaffer stands to give his opening statement. He starts with an affable smile on his face, but as soon as he starts to speak, he is all serious business.

"I am not going to stand here today and tell you that Jenny Nichols is guilty of murder. Clearly the state of New Jersey believes that to be the case, or you would not be sitting here in judgment of her.

"But that is for another day, actually for tomorrow. You will start to see the evidence that law enforcement has compiled, and you will weigh it carefully, and you will decide if it is sufficient to prove our case beyond a reasonable doubt.

"But if there is one thing I want to convince you of, it is that this day, in this courtroom, is like many thousands that have come before it in courtrooms all over this great country. It is, believe it or not, business as usual.

"Jenny Nichols is famous, you don't need me to tell you that. You've seen all the media coverage all these weeks; unless you were in a coma, there was no way to avoid it. You see the chaos outside the courthouse that you had to navigate to get in. They are selling T-shirts about this trial . . . heaven help us.

"But at the end of the day, Jenny Nichols is like anyone else. She is a human being entitled to the same presumption of innocence as every American citizen. She has her rights, and among those is the right to confront her accusers, to state her case, and be judged by you.

"But that presumption of innocence does not mean she is innocent. It means that the burden of the prosecution, in this case myself and my colleagues, is to convince you beyond a reasonable doubt that she is, in fact, guilty.

"Hard as it may be for you to believe, I have no dog in this fight. I, like you, seek to find and identify the truth. If a person is innocent, I want them to go free. And if they are guilty, I want them to pay for their crimes.

"All the attention focused on this case does not make it a difficult one. I actually believe, that after you see the facts and the evidence, that it will not be hard for you to reach a decision.

"Mr. Carpenter will tell you a story. He's already started to tell it, if you've read any of the press coverage leading up to this trial. It will not be rooted in fact, but will instead take hearsay and innuendo and *maybe*s and *could have been*s, and combine it all in a way to distract and confuse you.

"That is his right, and he is very good at it. So I caution you, focus on the facts, and only the facts. That is your job, and if you do it, as I know you will, then justice will be served. Thank you."

Shaffer takes his seat and Judge Slater asks whether I want to give my opening now or wait until we are about to present the defense case. As I do 100 percent of the time, I opt to go now.

The jury is going to be spending the upcoming days hearing the prosecution's side of things; I need to let them know that it is not the only side.

"Ladies and gentlemen, my name is Andy Carpenter, and I am the storyteller that Mr. Shaffer just warned you about. I listened as you did, and it sounded like his biggest fear was that you would not be smart enough to see through my trickery.

"I will admit that like every lawyer, there are times when I wished that I could fool the jurors, that I could just make up stuff and they would believe it and I could go home a winner. But you know what? The next time that actually happens will be the first. Because the system doesn't allow for it.

"If the facts are presented accurately and fairly, and in this case Judge Slater will assure that will be the case, then juries almost always make the right decisions. That's because lawyers like me and Mr. Shaffer only accept people to sit in judgment who are capable of it.

"Each of you passed that test, or you wouldn't be sitting here. So I hope we can stop with the nonsense, with the ominous warnings of evil, deceitful attorneys, and get on with the pursuit of the truth.

"The truth is that Jenny Nichols did not, could not, plunge a knife into the back of Ryan Griffin. It just simply never happened.

It goes against everything she stands for, against the way she has lived her entire life. It is not the way she is wired.

"Mr. Shaffer told you that at its core, this is like any other case. In one way he is right. Despite Ms. Nichols's fame, she should be treated like any other defendant. That's what she wants, and what I want.

"But I'll tell you one way in which this case is very different. Almost always, people in your position can only judge the guilt or innocence of a defendant. If you believe that person to be not guilty, you are left with the frustration of not knowing who actually committed the crime.

"That is always an unsatisfying outcome, since the crime will then likely go unpunished. That won't happen here. Not only will we demonstrate that Jenny Nichols did not commit this horrible crime, but we will tell you who did.

"And it won't be a story. It will be based on facts. Only facts. You will first hear the prosecution's side of things. Please reserve judgment until you hear both sides.

"Thank you for listening."

The Feds came in and took over the whole thing, including your boy," Pete Stanton says when he calls.

"Bondar is in federal custody?"

"According to the Suffern cops, yes. It's way out of my hands."

"What about making him for the three murders there?"

"The homicide cop in Suffern says they can make that case. They found forensic evidence tying him to it. But it would be a lot easier if he were in their control."

"Will you let me know if you hear anything else?" I ask.

"I live to serve you. Now you want to tell me the truth about how you learned about the three graves up there?"

"I told you; it was an anonymous tip. It came in on the tip line that we set up."

"So you got a tip on the tip line?"

"Correct. An anonymous one, cloaked in anonymity."

"And they anonymously decided to tell you about the three murders rather than tell the police?"

"Tip lines can be wonderful things," I say. "Heartwarming, actually. Yet anonymous."

"You're full of shit," Pete says.

"I am aware of that. Laurie considers it part of my charm."

Click.

I don't talk to Pete on the phone that often, but when I do, he usually forgets to say goodbye before he hangs up.

I am not at all happy that Bondar is under federal control. I was hoping that by the time we presented the defense case we would have much more information about Bondar that would come out of the murder investigation. In a perfect world, however unlikely, he would have ratted out his bosses to get a better legal outcome.

That ain't happening now.

Laurie and I don't talk about it over dinner, because we don't want to upset Jenny. But afterward, when Jenny heads to her room, we discuss it over a glass of wine.

"We don't have enough on Bondar to tie him to our case, or to Ryan Griffin," I say.

"You have the phone records of Griffin calling him."

"True. But that's a long way from pinning the murder on him. We haven't even come up with a reason why Bondar or his bosses, whoever they are, would have benefited from Griffin's death."

She nods. "And the records show Bondar's phone was not at the house that night."

"Right; that's a big problem, but not the biggest. The phone not being there doesn't mean that he wasn't. I can finesse that; maybe he had it turned off because he didn't want it to make noise while he snuck in. Or maybe he just forgot it; people can identify with that."

"Or maybe he turned it off so it couldn't be tracked," she says.

"Maybe, but he didn't do that in Suffern."

"True. So what's the bigger problem?" she asks.

"It doesn't fit with his style. He killed Hoffman anonymously in a hit-and-run. He took the security guys off to Suffern, killed them, and buried their bodies. He wasn't terribly careful about any of it, but it still doesn't jibe with the Griffin murder."

"Because of Jenny," she says.

"Right. He could have killed Griffin anywhere and not left a trace. Instead he chose to do it in Jenny's house, and take the time and care to frame her as the killer? Why the different tactic?"

"Maybe it was important to get Jenny out of the way?" she asks.

"He could have waited until she got home and set it up as a murder-suicide . . . a love affair gone off the rails. Griffin couldn't have her, so he killed her and then himself."

"You have a sick mind," Laurie says.

"I am very much aware of that. It's another part of my charm."

"You might want to hide some of that charm." Then, "What do you think we should tell Ricky when he gets home about why Jenny is living here?"

"Good question," I say. "If he asks, and he might not, we could just say that she's a friend from out of town. He knows her; she was here before he left. So we just say she didn't want to stay in a hotel, so we invited her to stay here."

"You think he'll buy that?"

"No," I say. "Because even at his age he'll see talk of it in the media, or hear about it from his friends at school. Plus, he'll wonder about that big bracelet on her ankle."

"How about if we try the truth?"

"The truth?" I ask. "That's an interesting concept; I'm just not that familiar with it."

"We tell him that she has been accused of something she didn't do, and that Daddy is helping her prove that she didn't."

"Okay . . . if you think so . . ."

"He can handle the truth, Andy. He's growing up; he's a teen-ager."

"Barely a teenager. Actually, if you round down, he's still twelve."

haffer's first witness is a 911 operator named Logan Owens.
The weird thing about that, at least from my perspective,
is that a stray dog that was once brought to the Tara Foundation
had a tag that identified the dog's name as Logan Owens. He had
been stray for a month, but we reunited him with his distraught
owner.

I don't believe in coincidences, but that's a beauty.

After Shaffer identifies what Owens does for a living, he asks
him, "Did you receive a phone call from the defendant, Jenny
Nichols?"

"I did, but at the time I didn't know her name."

"But you know it now?"

Owens smiles. "Oh, yes."

"What time did the call come in?"

"One thirty-one A.M."

"Was Ms. Nichols upset?"

I could object that the witness could not know how Jenny was
feeling, but I decide to let it pass. Shaffer would just amend the
question to limit it to Owens's assessment of how he sounded.
And none of it will matter, because I know they plan to play
the tape.

"She sounded upset, yes."

Shaffer introduces the tape as evidence and plays it for the
jury and the rest of us.

Owens: Nine-one-one emergency. What is your situation?

Jenny: There's someone in my kitchen. I think he's dead. . . .
  I'm sure he is.

Owens: Do you know what happened to him?

Jenny: There's blood everywhere. And a knife . . .

Owens: I am sending the police to you now. Is there anyone else
  on the premises?

Jenny: No. Just me.

Owens: Are you certain of that?

Jenny: Oh, God . . . this can't be happening.

Owens: Are you certain that there is no one else there?

Jenny: Yes, I'm certain. I've been asleep.

Owens: This happened while you were sleeping?

Jenny: Yes, it must have. I mean, I don't know.

Owens: Do you know the deceased?

Jenny: Yes . . . his name is Ryan Griffin. I didn't know he
  was here. There's blood everywhere . . . this is horrible.

Owens: The police will be there momentarily.

As he says that, we hear noises in the background.

Jenny: They're here. I see the lights.
Owens: Open the door and let them in.
Jenny: I will.

That ends the tape. I don't think it was particularly damaging to us; it's not in any way inconsistent with our defense. Shaffer just played it to set the scene.

There's nothing else for Shaffer to ask Owens; the only connection to the case that Owens had was the conversation that we have all just heard.

I decide not to cross-examine the witness. I usually like to score at least some points so the jury won't forget that the defense exists, but Owens did no damage at all, and the tape speaks for itself.

Jenny did sound upset. Shaffer will ultimately spin it that she was upset because she had murdered someone and was afraid of the consequences. My view is that anyone who found a dead person stabbed to death in their kitchen would be upset; not to react that way would be bizarre.

Next up for the prosecution is Sergeant Derek Sylvester. He was the highest-ranking officer in the group that was first to arrive on the scene.

"Sergeant Sylvester, you received notification of the nine-one-one call that night?"

"I did. I went to the scene with other officers immediately."

"How soon after being notified were you there?"

"Three and a half minutes."

"What did you do when you arrived?"

"We checked to confirm that the victim was deceased, which he was. At the same time other officers went through the house to make sure that no one else was there."

"Where was Ms. Nichols when you arrived?"

"She had heard us pull up and opened the door for us. She directed us to the kitchen."

"Did she follow you in there?"

"Yes. I then instructed her to go outside with one of the other officers."

"Did you first ask her what had happened?" Shaffer asks.

"I did. She claimed not to know. Said she just walked in and discovered the body."

"What happened next?"

"We confirmed that the house was secure and waited for homicide to arrive. We then turned the scene over to them and went outside to secure the perimeter from any onlookers."

"Were there many such onlookers?"

"None that I saw. It's a very secluded neighborhood, and it was the middle of the night."

This time I have a few questions on cross-examination. "Sergeant, you said that Ms. Nichols met you at the front door and went with you to the kitchen?"

"Yes."

"Did you pass the staircase leading to the second floor on the way?"

"I did. The bottom of the staircase is maybe ten feet from the front door."

"The bedrooms are on the second floor, is that correct? If you know . . ."

"They are."

"How far is the kitchen from the front door?"

"I guess . . . maybe sixty feet. Maybe more."

"It's a large house?" I ask.

"Yes. And the kitchen is toward the back."

"So if someone walked into that house through the front door and went directly up to a bedroom, they would not pass the kitchen?"

"They would not."

"Thank you. No further questions."

Sergeant Sylvester is another witness that did not hurt us, and actually helped us preview our defense.

The upcoming witnesses won't be so kind.

've been so focused on Bondar that I haven't paid enough attention to Audrey Dodge.

The truth is that if central casting were going to send down a suspect in the Ryan Griffin murder, Audrey Dodge would be a damn good fit.

She was Griffin's ex-wife, and by all accounts she was dumped by him after he spent a good deal of time cheating on her. The humiliation of that was compounded by the fact that it was well reported in the press, due to Griffin's celebrity.

Lieutenant Drummond in Los Angeles told me that Audrey's father, Carl Dodge, started his producing career using money supplied by a crime boss named Angelo Ricci. His belief was that the relationship had continued over the years, and Dodge was very tied into the mob.

The word is that Audrey and her father became estranged, but that does not mean the word is correct, nor does it mean that she could not have inherited the mob relationship despite her eventual separation from her father.

But the main reason we should be thinking more about Audrey Dodge as a person of interest is a business one. Our belief is that the production company, soon to become a streaming company, is operating fraudulently as a conduit for money laundering. We believe that Bondar's actions are in service of that conspiracy.

When Ryan Griffin was killed, Audrey Dodge moved into his position as a co-head of that company. She, more than anyone that we know of, directly profited from his disappearance from the scene.

I also asked Audrey if she had heard of Bondar, and it was soon after that he started targeting me. It's possible he knew about me because he saw us visit the security company in the Bronx, but the comment to Audrey might have been the final straw.

Add to all this the fact that Jenny's assistant, Linda Ivers, heard Audrey and Griffin angrily arguing the day before he died, and it's obvious that the motives for murder just keep on comin'.

Jenny could provide some insight to this, so one night I ask her what the relationship was between Audrey and Griffin.

"Not terrible," she says. "Audrey knew what Ryan was, and she had come to terms with it a while ago."

"She didn't resent the way he treated her?"

"I'm sure she did when it happened, and it may have lingered, but there comes a time you have to move on, you know? Otherwise it destroys you. She and I talked about it a lot, and I think she understood that. At least that's what she said."

"Did she warn you about him?" I ask.

She laughs. "Oh, yes. But I didn't listen, not at first. Ryan could be very charming."

"Did she ever visit you in the Englewood Cliffs house?" I ask.

"Yes. When she first came east to work on the production, I told her there was a house down the block that was renting out as an Airbnb. She thought she might like to stay away from the hubbub of the city. So she came out here to see what it was like. She decided it was too quiet, and too far to commute every day."

"But she was in the house, and maybe would have noticed that you didn't always lock the doors? Or that you sometimes left windows open?"

"Andy, there's no way Audrey killed Ryan. She could never do that. Why would she?"

"Maybe she wouldn't," I say. "But somebody did."

My conversation with Jenny didn't convince me that Audrey couldn't be a viable suspect. If anything, it strengthened my suspicion of her. Audrey's knowledge of the house for having been there, and her knowledge that Jenny sometimes didn't lock her doors made her a decent candidate.

Also, Bondar's existence is not inconsistent with that theory. Bondar was hired help, deadly hired help, and could have been employed either by the production company or by those supplying the money.

Audrey could have been calling the shots, and Bondar could have been acting on her behalf.

I will admit that I don't see Audrey as a mass murderer, but things could have gotten out of her control. And if she committed the actual act, and not Bondar, then it would tend to explain the differences in method.

Audrey might have considered it important to set up someone else as the killer, while Bondar wouldn't. So a lot of it fits logically, but proving it is another matter altogether.

Sam comes over to give me an update on what he has been doing. He brings along Larry Hoffman's computer, which he had gotten from Pam Sparaco, Larry's fiancée and beneficiary.

"What did you learn?" I ask.

"I'm afraid nothing that will help you. He did not seem like the type to include anything sensitive in emails or texts. The guy was obviously paranoid."

Sparaco had described him the same way; at the end she said he always thought he was being watched. "Why do you say that?"

"He was very afraid of being hacked. There were a lot of

Google searches about it, and he had just installed a very high-level protective software."

"But no hint as to why he feared hacking?"

"No. But here's a report I drew up of everything on the computer, including his search records for the two weeks before he died. It's in here, with the media articles." He takes a large envelope out of his briefcase and gives it to me.

"What media articles?"

"You asked me to monitor media stories about that new streaming service, Elite. These are just printed-out copies of some of the stories I found online."

"Right. Thanks, Sam."

"I hope you're not investing in that thing."

"I'm not, believe me. But why do you say that?"

"I hang out in some of these internet tech chat rooms. Some of the people in there are really connected in that world. I mean, with some of the top companies."

"So?"

"So this guy that Elite got to head up their IT operations, James Richards. The word is that he is, to put it kindly, not the right man for the job."

"Which means what?"

"You know how complicated it is to run a streaming service? Can you imagine how much Netflix spends on it? If it fails, you have no company. No one thinks Richards is up to it."

"Good," I say. "I hope they fail."

ergeant Tina Hatfield is in the forensics division and was the
S technician on the scene the night of Ryan Griffin's murder.

I have never dealt with her before because she doesn't practice
in Passaic County, but I have checked her out and she is said to
be competent and unflappable on the stand.

I hate people like that.

Shaffer calls her as his first witness today, and unlike the previous witnesses, her testimony will be damaging to Jenny.

"Sergeant Hatfield, you were in charge of the forensics team
at the murder scene?" Shaffer asks.

"I was."

Shaffer tells the jury that he is going to show photos from the
scene on the large screen mounted on the jury side of the courtroom. He warns them that some might be graphic in nature, and
apologizes for that in advance, even though everybody knows it's
intentional.

The first photograph is of the kitchen table. There are two
cups and saucers and two plates on the table, with a half-eaten
cake in the center. In the background can be seen Griffin's lower
body on the floor, with blood pooled around him.

"Is this the kitchen table as you found it?"

"Yes."

"Did you test the cups for fingerprints and DNA?"

"I did. The cup on the left had Ms. Nichols's fingerprints, and the one on the right had Mr. Griffin's prints.

"What about DNA?"

"Ms. Nichols's DNA was on the rim of the cup, where it would be from sipping the coffee."

"Did you search the entire house for fingerprints?"

"Yes, we found prints belonging to Ms. Nichols throughout the house, and Mr. Griffin's prints only in the kitchen. We also found Mr. Griffin's prints on the outside front door handle."

"Was the lock tampered with?"

"No."

"No one else's prints anywhere?"

"No. We inquired and learned that a housekeeper had been there the previous day, so it's likely that any other prints were wiped away."

Shaffer moves from item to item rapidly, showing relevant photographs and making his points quickly and effectively. "There was obviously a great deal of blood on the kitchen floor. Was it all Mr. Griffin's?"

"It was."

"Did you find his blood anywhere else?"

"Yes. There were traces in the sink drain . . . and—"

Shaffer interrupts. "Consistent with someone washing that blood off their hands?"

"Could be, yes. And we also found some blood on Ms. Nichols's clothing."

After getting Hatfield to identify the cake knife as the murder weapon, he turns the witness over to me. I have a great deal to try to accomplish, because each one of her revelations by itself could be devastating.

"Sergeant Hatfield, you said that Mr. Griffin's fingerprints were on one of the coffee cups, and Ms. Nichols's prints were on the other."

"Yes."

"And you said that Ms. Nichols must have sipped the coffee because her DNA was on the rim of one cup, but you didn't mention finding any DNA on the rim of the other cup. Is that because there was none there?"

"We did not find any . . . that's correct."

"Is it possible to sip coffee without leaving a DNA trace?" I ask.

"Highly unlikely."

"So unless someone stood over Mr. Griffin and poured the coffee into his mouth from a distance, he didn't have any?"

"I can't be certain."

"So you can be certain Ms. Nichols had some, but you lose your certainty when it comes to Mr. Griffin?" I don't wait for an answer; instead I ask that the photo of the table be brought up and Sergeant Hatfield to look at it.

"How much coffee was left in the cup with Mr. Griffin's prints?"

"Very little," she says.

"Maybe one swallow's worth?"

"Probably."

"Have you ever known anyone to pour only that much into a cup?"

"I couldn't say."

"Couldn't or wouldn't?"

Shaffer objects that I'm being argumentative. Duhhh. Judge Slater sustains. I've made my point, so I move on.

"Sergeant, changes happen to a body at death, do they not?"

"Of course."

"Breathing stops, et cetera, right?"

"Yes."

"Do fingerprints get removed?"

"What do you mean?" she asks.

I hold up my hand. "I have fingerprints on each of these fingers. If I were to die, right now, would those prints leave my hand? Would they go blank and smooth?"

"No."

"So if I were lying here dead, and you had something in your hand . . . say, for argument purposes, a coffee cup . . . you could press it onto my fingers and it would leave a print?"

"Yes."

"Just as if I were alive?"

"Yes."

"Now I'd like to offer a hypothetical, and tell me if this is possible, please. A person comes into the room, and sees a friend on the floor, with a substantial amount of blood on them. Is it possible that person might go over to the person on the floor and check on them? Maybe see if they are alive?"

"It's possible."

"Could that person have gotten a small amount of blood on their hands, and maybe on their clothes?"

"We don't know that that's what happened here," Hatfield says.

"Are you not familiar with the word *hypothetical*?" I ask.

She's obviously annoyed, so I continue. "If this person had not checked on their friend, would you have found that unusual?"

"That depends."

"Oh, I didn't realize that showing concern for a friend could be a bad thing." I frown my disbelief at the answers I'm getting.

I continue. "Now, continuing the hypothetical, if the person who came into the room was not a police officer, but was a person who had never encountered a situation like this before, is it possible he or she might have wanted to wash the blood off their hands?"

"It's possible."

"Thank you. No further questions."

I sit down, not really satisfied with the results, even though it is the best I could have hoped for. I got the witness to say that our explanation was possible, but everybody in the room, jury included, knows it's not likely.

After court is over, I play some messages on my phone that came in during the day. One is from FBI Special Agent Douglas Haigler. He says that he wants to talk to me about Sergey Bondar, and is hoping to do so after the court session today.

I call the number back and get his voice mail. I tell him that he can meet me at my office at 5 P.M. No need to call back; I will be there either way.

I hope he shows; I have a lot of questions for him.

Special Agent Haigler is right on time, showing up at 5 P.M., walking by the fruit stand and trudging upstairs.

He walks into my office, looks around at my pathetic surroundings, and says, "You're a big-time attorney?"

"They don't come any bigger."

He frowns. "I can't believe this place."

"Thank you. I think it's important to show the trappings of success. It's expensive, but worth it. That lamp alone was almost thirty bucks."

"I almost tripped over a cantaloupe downstairs," he says.

"It's a risk I take every day. The pineapples are even worse; don't try walking through there barefoot. You want a Diet Coke? It's all I have."

"No thanks." I sit beside my desk and he sits in the chair across from it. "As I said in my message, I want to talk about Sergey Bondar."

"Good. So do I. What made you think he was connected to your case?"

"My client is wrongly accused of killing Ryan Griffin. Bondar killed the three security guards assigned to Griffin, and Larry Hoffman."

"Who is Larry Hoffman?"

I frown. "Have you guys been on vacation? Look him up . . . Google should help."

"What made you think that Bondar killed the security guards?"

"We received an anonymous tip."

"You know it's illegal to lie to an FBI agent?"

"I've heard that. It's very frightening."

"I talked to Pete Stanton. He told me you'd say it was a tip."

"If nothing else, you have to admire my consistency," I say.

"He also told me you were a pain in the ass."

"I refer you to my previous comment about my consistency."

He nods and then switches to his *I'm in the FBI so cut the crap* tone. "Tell me why you think he is involved in your case, why he might have killed those people. It will help in our investigation, which can't be bad for anyone. And if we come up with anything that will help you, it's yours."

"Why does it matter to you? You can make him for the security guard deaths, and he's already wanted by Interpol. This is not exactly a head scratcher."

"We know the *who*," he says. "We are worried about the *why*. And our preference would be to deal with him here, and not extradite him."

"I wish I knew the *why* myself; it's the key to our case," I say, but I know I have to give him more. "Okay, here's what I believe. Bondar was representing people, probably an oligarch named Miranov, who was laundering money through a company in Hollywood."

I notice a slight reaction from Haigler when I say Miranov, but he doesn't interrupt, so I continue. "That company is now run by Griffin's former partner, Arnold Chrisman, and Griffin's ex-wife, Audrey Dodge. They just announced a streaming service called Elite, which will require even more money than a guy like Miranov could likely provide. It would take Putin-level money."

"Why do you think they killed Griffin?" he asks. "How would that have helped them?"

"That's the key question, and I can't answer it. He had a drug problem, so maybe he was behaving erratically and that scared them, but I think it was something more than that." Then, "What is it you're worried about?"

"What do you mean?" he asks.

"I mean Bondar's a killer and you caught him. You could turn him over to Interpol and get him off your plate. Or New York State could put him away for the Suffern guard killings. He doesn't have to be your problem, yet you're sitting here. Why is that?"

"Miranov," he says. "He's not just laundering money . . . he thinks bigger than that. That helps him, but he always goes for a two-for-one. Laundering is the one; it's the two that worries us."

"And Bondar is not talking?"

"He actually is, but selectively. He would rather be dealt with here than extradited."

"What is he saying?"

"He's copped to killing the security guards, but won't go near anything to do with Miranov."

"What about the Griffin murder?"

"He denies it. Which does not mean he didn't do it; it just means he has some reason for not going there. Maybe he's afraid it would somehow implicate Miranov. Miranov is not a guy to mess with."

"I need to make him for the Griffin murder," I say.

Haigler frowns. "Maybe he's your man, but I don't see how a movie company ties into this. It's not like Miranov wants to spread propaganda. He thinks a lot bigger than that. He's about making money, and destroying things if necessary to do so."

Haigler leaves after we promise each other to trade any information we get. Neither of us will keep our promise if it hurts our respective positions, and we both understand that.

I'm troubled by a couple of things that Haigler said. The most obvious is that Bondar has willingly confessed to murders, but won't admit to killing Griffin. The second is his view that this can't be just about making movies, or streaming them. If it's not, then we have no case.

We are going to have to make the jury see who Bondar is, and what he has done, and hope that it creates at least reasonable doubt in the jury's mind about Jenny's role in this. We have to make them understand that it is absurd to think that Jenny could have been involved with someone like that.

If Bondar was out there killing people, isn't it reasonable to consider that he might have killed Griffin?

Dakota Graves has been flown in by Shaffer as the next prosecution witness.

She is an actress who lives in Los Angeles and is one of Jenny's closest friends. It is clear from her body language that she is not happy to be here, or at least that's how she wants it to appear.

She doesn't look at Jenny as she walks to the stand, which is never a good sign. Shaffer has her identify who she is, including her occupation and where she lives.

"Do you consider yourself a friend of the defendant, Jenny Nichols?"

"I do. A very close friend. I hope I still am after today."

"How long have you known her?"

"Almost twenty years."

"And you are open with each other? Do you have the kind of relationship where you confide in each other?"

"Yes, I believe so," she says. "I certainly tell Jenny everything, and she shares things with me as well."

"Do you remember a time when Jenny was dating Ryan Griffin?"

"Of course."

"She spoke to you about their relationship?"

She nods. "Yes, many times."

"Was there a point that she was happy in that relationship?"

"Oh, yes. Ryan really went all out to win her over. He could be very charming. And for a while it worked."

"But then it stopped, as you put it, *working,*" Shaffer asks.

"Yes."

"Why did that happen? If you know . . ."

"Ryan was cheating on her," she says. "Friends saw him with other women. He wasn't even that discreet about it."

"That surprised her?"

"It did. I don't think it should have; that was his reputation. But it definitely surprised her. She believed Ryan when he said he would never hurt her like that."

"Did it anger her?"

She hesitates, and looks at Jenny, as if wishing she could be anywhere else but in this courtroom. "It did. I never saw Jenny so angry."

"She talked about it?"

Another hesitation, then, "Yes."

"What did she say?"

"That she was either going to dump him or kill him."

"Thank you. No further questions."

I stand up to cross-examine, and I have to admit I am annoyed with the witness. She's trying to come across as reluctant to be hurting her friend, but she did not have to let it be known that Jenny had said that to her. Had she kept her mouth shut, Shaffer wouldn't have called her to testify in the first place.

With friends like her . . .

"Ms. Graves, what did the police say when you told them about your friend's comment about killing Mr. Griffin?" I ask.

She looks confused. "I didn't call the police."

"Ms. Nichols threatened to kill someone and you didn't think that was worthy of telling the police?"

"No."

"Did you warn Mr. Griffin that his life was in danger?"

"No."

"You weren't worried about his safety?"

"No."

"Why is that? Who did you think was going to protect him?"

"I didn't think he needed protection. I didn't think Jenny was serious."

"You didn't? Why not?"

"Because I know her; she could never kill anyone."

"When you originally spoke with Mr. Shaffer or his people, did you tell them that you did not think she was serious? That the Jenny Nichols you know could not kill anyone?"

"Yes, I'm sure I did."

I shake my head in fake amazement at how Shaffer could have tried such a trick.

"Have you ever seen Ms. Nichols angry before?" I ask.

"Of course. Many times."

"Are you aware of her ever being violent?"

"No."

"Never threatened anyone with a knife?"

"No."

"Did she ever babysit for your child?"

"Yes."

"So you trusted her?"

"Of course. She's my friend."

"Did Ms. Nichols ever talk about Mr. Griffin's drug use?"

"Yes. She said it was getting worse, and that he was acting erratically."

"Was she worried about him?"

"Yes. She said she told him to get help, but he said he didn't need any, that he was fine."

"You testified that she said she was either going to dump Mr. Griffin or kill him. Is that correct?"

"That's what she said."

"Did she dump him?"

"Yes."

"No further questions."

Ricky's flight is due in from San Francisco at six thirty.

Laurie picked me up and we got to Newark Airport at five fifteen. If I didn't have to be in court today, I probably would have gotten here last night . . . that's how anxious I am to see him.

In every phone call and email we've gotten from him, it has sounded like he's having a great time. By all indications the trip was properly supervised and the kids were well taken care of; it will no doubt be a summer to remember.

But I'm still nervous. I want the old Ricky; I have this irrational fear that he'll have changed. Not for the worse . . . just changed. I'm not big on change when it comes to family.

I'm afraid he'll get off the plane and introduce us to his wife, or tell us he has a job, or want to be driven to his new apartment. Or maybe he'll want to drive himself.

I've got some issues. Or, as Laurie put it, "Andy, you've got some issues."

We're in the waiting area when the information flashes on the board that the plane has landed. That's a good first step.

There are televisions in the room, and I see that on CNN Arnold Chrisman is being interviewed by a business reporter. I can't hear what they're saying, but the chyron announces that Elite will be officially online in ten days.

Whether intentionally or not, they are capitalizing on the

publicity that the murder trial has generated. A start-up of this kind would simply not be that big a deal, nor would it be worthy of this coverage, if not for our case.

I can't say I blame them. It's a competitive industry, and they are not overtly invoking Griffin's name and memory. Of course, they don't have to; the media is doing that for them. I wouldn't be surprised if it results in a larger group of initial subscribers than would have otherwise materialized. Whether those people will stay with the service remains to be seen, and will probably depend on the programming offered.

And suddenly Ricky is here. The man from Rein Teen Tours confirms that we are his parents, and we get greeting hugs. Ricky then runs off to say goodbye to his friends, including new ones he's made during the trip.

Laurie's eyes are teary, but it's hard to see clearly through my own wet eyes. Must be my allergies.

The goodbyes take a while, and all the kids trade phone numbers and email addresses. But finally we collect the bags, go to the car, and head home.

I'm still a little nervous about how we are going to explain Jenny's presence in the house. Laurie thinks we should just tell the truth, that he is mature enough to deal with it, but I want to couch it in gentle terms.

On the way home, Ricky regales us with stories about the trip. His favorite stops were Yosemite and Las Vegas, which I guess means he's a combination of Laurie and me. Then, from out of nowhere, he asks, "How's the Nichols case going?"

"What?" I ask, since I can't think of anything else to say. It also annoys me that Laurie is smiling.

"You know, Jenny's trial. How is it going?"

"Fine," I say. "It's going fine."

"Joey Senack thinks she's guilty and that you're going to lose.

I told him he's crazy, that I know her and she didn't do it. And that you would prove it."

"Joey Senack is wrong," Laurie says. "And you're right."

Ricky smiles knowingly. "I knew it. I can't wait until you win and I can tell Joey, *I told you so.*"

As if I didn't have enough pressure, now I have Joey Senack to worry about.

J anet Campbell, Shaffer's next witness, is a waitress who was assigned to serve us in the upstairs room at Charlie's the night we had our dinner party.

She witnessed what had happened when Ryan Griffin showed up with Danny and Gurley. With my permission, Vince had written about it after Jenny was arrested.

Once Shaffer establishes the time and place, Shaffer asks, "Who was at the dinner?"

"Well, Ms. Nichols, Mr. Carpenter and his wife, and some friends of theirs. I didn't know their names. Except for Mr. Sanders; he is at Charlie's very often, so I know him."

"Was there a point at which Ryan Griffin came into the room?"

"Yes, I would say about a half hour after Ms. Nichols got there."

"What did he do when he arrived?"

"He went over to Ms. Nichols and demanded that she leave with him."

"What did she say?"

"That she wouldn't go, and that he should leave."

"Did he leave?"

"Not right away. He reached out and grabbed her arm, and then Laurie, Mr. Carpenter's wife, twisted his arm and pushed him down to the table."

Shaffer has a big smile on his face. "Did Mr. Carpenter do anything?"

"He said something, but I don't remember what."

The jury and everyone else in the courtroom laughs, except of course for me.

"What happened next?"

"Two men that were with Mr. Griffin, they tried to help him, but two of the men at the party stopped them. They stopped them really hard."

"What happened next?"

"The men left, and someone asked if Ms. Nichols was alright . . . if they could help her."

"What did she say?"

"That she didn't need help; that she could handle him . . . Mr. Griffin, I mean."

"Did she seem angry to you?"

I object, but Judge Slater overrules and lets Campbell answer.

"Yes, she seemed very angry. She said she could handle it, and that it wasn't the first time something like that had happened. Then she said *damn him*."

It's an interesting move by Shaffer. He's willing to paint Griffin as a bad guy, in order to give Jenny a motive to kill him. His point will obviously be that it's not okay to murder someone, whether or not they are a nice person.

It would play into our hands if we were claiming self-defense. We could say that Griffin went to Jenny's house and elevated the level of abuse, and she killed him to defend herself. But we're not saying that; we are taking the position that it was someone else entirely who plunged the knife into his back.

It also leaves me with little to accomplish on cross. Campbell has correctly described what happened, so accurately that she must have been taking notes. So I'm going to focus on a specific area of her testimony, after a few brief questions.

"Ms. Campbell, did Ms. Nichols react calmly to what happened when Mr. Griffin came in?"

"Yes, I would say so."

"She was able to control her anger?"

"Definitely. If it was me I would have freaked out."

Shaffer asks that the remark be stricken, but the judge overrules the objection.

"You said there were two men with Mr. Griffin. What was your impression of them? Did they seem like friends of his?"

"No, they were dressed in these suits, you know, like they were bouncers at a club. They were big guys, and they stayed behind him a few steps. But when Laurie grabbed Mr. Griffin, they moved forward."

"So they were like security guards, there to protect him?" As I ask the question, I'm reminded that when we questioned them, Gurley said they were assigned to *watch* Griffin. I thought that was a strange word to use then, and I still do.

"Yes, that's what it seemed like."

"Are those two men in the courtroom today?"

"No."

"Have you seen them since that night?"

Shaffer jumps up as if someone set his chair on fire. "Your Honor, may we approach?"

Shaffer and I go up for a bench conference, and Shaffer says that this is an obvious attempt for me to introduce information about the subsequent murder of the two men. "It is outside the scope of the direct examination," he says.

He's right, but I take a shot and say, "Your Honor, Mr. Shaffer asked about the men and opened the door."

Judge Slater thinks for a moment and says, "The door was not opened. You can attempt to introduce information about them in your defense case, Mr. Carpenter, and at that time I will make a ruling as to admissibility."

I wrap up my questioning of the witness. "Ms. Campbell, did the dinner go on for a while after Mr. Griffin left?"

"Oh yes, for almost three hours."

"Did Ms. Nichols still seem angry during that time?"

"Oh no. She was smiling and seemed like she was having fun."

"Thank you."

It is really nice having Ricky home.

We're settling into our old routines . . . having breakfast together, him going with me when I walk the dogs, et cetera. Ricky always holds Sebastian's leash because there is no danger that Sebastian will pull free and run off.

It's like walking a barking turtle.

I go into his room after dinner tonight to renew our video football game challenge. Ricky keeps a record, and I am currently behind forty-seven games to three. I actually don't remember the three victories; I think he's giving me credit if I come close.

But tonight cold reality sets in. When I get to Ricky's room, he's already playing the game. Mamie, who has really taken to Ricky, sits in his lap, and he pets her as he plays. She has been loving having so many dogs and humans to play with.

"I'm playing Jerry Magnes," Ricky says. "He's my friend from the tour."

"You don't have to be in the same room?"

Ricky frowns. "Dad . . ." If he had finished the sentence, it would have been, *Dad, you're a dinosaur, you know?*

Yes, Ricky, I know.

"What if he's just pretending to be Jerry? What if he's some kind of weirdo?"

"We chat while we play. If he's a weirdo, he was a weirdo on the tour with me, because he knows everything we did."

"Okay, just call me if you want an easy win."

I was hoping to use a father-son video game to delay my going into the den and doing more witness preparation. But I get a mini reprieve when Sam calls.

"Got anything for me to do?" Sam asks. "Things have really slowed down."

"Nothing I can think of. Actually, maybe there is. You told me that the only phones at the house that night were Griffin's and Jenny's."

"Right."

"Are you positive Bondar's wasn't there?"

"I can never be absolutely positive, but I'm pretty sure. I can look again if you want."

"Please do. It would be huge for our case if he was there."

"I'm on it," Sam says. Then, "Did you see that Elite thing is going online next week?"

"Yes."

"They're going to crash and burn."

"Why do you say that?"

"Because you can't put an operation like that together so fast, especially with the team they've assembled. And once they crash, they're history."

"Why?"

"Because that kind of business is about trust. You pay for a subscription and they better provide service . . . and I'm talking about every time. Once you let people down, they never forget."

"Maybe they'll surprise you."

"I don't think so. I'll get back to you on Bondar's phone that night, but you're not going to like the answer."

"I understand. Thanks, Sam."

I get off the phone and head for the den. The truth is I could not care less if Elite crashes and burns like Sam says. I'd probably rather they did; if they're going to launder money they might as well lose some in the process.

But their success or failure as a streaming service is well down on my list of concerns. If the list was single spaced, it would be on page two . . . near the bottom.

Captain Richard Jansing of the New Jersey State Police is Shaffer's last witness.

He was the lead detective on the case, and was on the scene the night of the murder. His role is to put a bow on the prosecution's case, though it is tied up pretty well already.

Shaffer puts another photograph up depicting the scene; he just loves showing it. If his photos could be gorier, he would love it even more. He wants the jury to recoil from Jenny and despise her for doing such a thing.

"Is this the scene exactly as it was when you arrived?"

Jansing nods. "Yes, it is."

"You are familiar with the coroner's report?"

"Yes."

I could object and insist that the coroner comment on his own report, but I've read it repeatedly, and if Jansing mischaracterizes it I will pounce on him. It won't happen, but if it did, I would rather allege that he is biased than the coroner.

"What was the estimate for how long Mr. Griffin was dead until the time of the nine-one-one call?"

"Between three and four hours."

"Mr. Griffin's head was the closest part of his body to the table. What does that tell you about his position when stabbed?"

"He was just standing in place, not running from his accuser."

"Why do you say that?"

"Well for one thing, he was facing the sink. There would be no logical reason to run to the sink as a means of escape. Secondly, if he were moving forward, his head would have fallen forward. That is especially true since he was stabbed in the upper back."

"So you think he was unsuspecting? That he had no sense he was about to be killed?"

"I can't be sure, of course, but that is how I read it. It appears that he was having coffee, stood up and moved toward the sink, or maybe the drawers next to it, and was surprised from behind."

"Was death instant?" Shaffer asks.

"The medical examiner says that the stab wound would not in itself have been fatal, but that Mr. Griffin bled out."

"So the killer struck and then watched while he bled to death?"

"I can't say that from personal knowledge," Jansing says. "The killer could have left the room."

"Do you know how Mr. Griffin got to the house that night?"

"I do not. He could have been dropped off by his security people; there is no record of him taking a cab, but if he hailed a yellow cab in New York City, that ride may not have been recorded."

When it's my turn, I begin with, "Captain Jansing, could this scene have been staged?"

"What do you mean?"

"I mean, could the killer have struck and then made it look like Ms. Nichols was responsible? Is there anything about it that struck you as strange?"

"I see no evidence of staging, and nothing struck me as strange. The pieces all seemed to fit."

"How convenient," I say. "There was testimony earlier that while Mr. Griffin's fingerprints were on the coffee cup, there was no DNA showing he had sipped any."

"I'm aware of that."

"Yet there was only a small amount of coffee left in the cup. Can you explain that?"

"No, I can't. That happens in these investigations. Obviously, there is always an explanation, but it's sometimes not detectable after the fact."

"Do you see the coffee maker in this photograph?" I hold it up so both he and the jury can see it.

"Yes."

"Is it a Keurig? The type that makes one cup per pod?"

"Yes."

"According to the discovery, the records prepared by your department, there was a used pod in the machine, but no used pods in the garbage or anywhere else in the kitchen."

"So?"

"So two people sat for coffee but only used one pod? When there was a bowl full of unused ones right next to the machine?"

"Apparently."

"Is this another one of those things that can't be explained, and happens in investigations like this?"

"Apparently."

"Here's a possible hypothetical. Ms. Nichols had coffee earlier in the evening, and left her DNA on the cup. Then the killer created the second setting, to make it look like Mr. Griffin joined her. Is that possible?"

"There's no evidence of that."

"Did you find fingerprints on the knife?"

"No."

"Another thing that can't be explained in investigations like this?"

"Killers often wipe their prints off murder weapons."

"So they try to conceal their involvement by wiping their prints off of the murder weapon but they leave the victim's prints all over the room, and then leave the victim lying on the floor of their kitchen and then alert the police? Is that what killers often do?"

"Murderers do not always behave rationally."

"As part of your investigation, did you talk to people to ascertain Ms. Nichols's character and history?"

"To a degree, yes."

"That's how you came to find her friend Ms. Graves and fly her in from Los Angeles, isn't that correct?" I ask.

"Yes."

"Please tell the jury about all the times you learned of violence in Ms. Nichols's past. I don't mean stabbings or attempted murders, I mean any violence at all."

"We did not learn of any."

"You said that murderers often behave irrationally, so please list the irrational acts you've learned that Ms. Nichols has on her past record. Things that people told you."

"There were none."

"So a person with absolutely no violence in their history, and no tendency toward irrational acts, stabbed someone in the back, watched him bleed to death, went to sleep for three hours, and then called the police so they could find the body in her kitchen? That's your theory of the case?"

"It is."

I shake my head. "Then I agree. There are some things about police investigations that cannot be explained. No further questions."

Shaffer objects, but I am already back seated at the defense table when Judge Slater strikes my last comment from the record.

The next words I hear are Shaffer's. "Your Honor, the prosecution rests."

Since Shaffer rested his case midafternoon on Friday, Judge Slater says that we will reconvene for the defense case to begin on Monday.

On the one hand I was not pleased by that; it gives the jurors three days to ponder all the things they've heard that were negative for our side. On the other hand, we were not exactly going to wow them in the two hours left on Friday.

This gives me an entire weekend to wish that we had a more effective case. We are basically in the same place we have been in for a while. We have no ability to conclusively prove that Jenny did not commit this crime. We can only go for reasonable doubt by offering an alternative killer.

Which is where Bondar comes in.

I'm confident that Judge Slater will have to admit testimony relating to Bondar; I can present enough connections between him and Ryan Griffin to ensure that. What I don't have is a reason for the violent actions Bondar was taking, and more important, I lack a reason for him to have eliminated Griffin.

We have made absolutely no progress in proving that there is money laundering going on at Griffin Entertainment or Elite, the soon-to-be-launched streaming service. Miranov, the oligarch who employs Bondar, certainly is capable of it, and I firmly believe that's what's going on. But not only can't I come close to proving it to the jury, there's no way Judge Slater will even let me allege it.

FBI special agent Haigler admitted he was worried about Miranov being in this for something more than money laundering. I still don't know what that could be, and if he has figured it out, he's reneged on his promise to tell me.

I also still believe that Audrey Dodge is a significant player in all of this, and I've tried calling her three times to set up another interview. She hasn't taken any of my calls, so I've left messages, but the fourth one is the charm, sort of. . . .

She gets on the phone and starts with, "Mr. Carpenter, I am really busy, and I told you everything I know when we met."

"I've learned a lot more since then," I say. "This time I'll ask different questions."

"We're talking now; a meeting is not going to happen. What kind of questions do you have for me?"

"Well, for example, I might ask you about the argument you had with Ryan Griffin."

She laughs, which surprises me. "Which one? We had a different one every day."

"This was the day before he died."

"So you think that I had an argument with Ryan and then killed him? Goodbye, Mr. Carpenter. Wish Jenny good luck for me; with your theories, she's going to need it."

"You take care now," I say. "We can talk after you get the subpoena."

I hang up, thoroughly pissed off.

I may or may not ultimately call her to testify, but I want a subpoena to make her uncomfortable about her potential appearance in court and worried about what she might be asked. Maybe she'll make a mistake that I can use against her. My rooting for things like that shows what trouble we are in.

I'm in my den reading through case documents on Saturday afternoon when Jenny comes in. "Andy, can I talk to you for a minute?"

"Sure."

"I sense that we're in an uphill fight. Am I right?"

"We have a decent chance," I say. "We have a good story to tell the jury."

"But you wish we had more?"

I smile. "There has never been a case where I didn't wish I had more."

"Well, I think you've done a great job."

"Bill Parcells used to say, *You are what your record says you are.*"

"Meaning?" she asks.

"Meaning I'll have only done a great job if we win."

She nods. "I have only one more question. Who is Bill Parcells?"

Is she serious? Who is Bill Parcells, the greatest coach in the history of the New York Giants? A two-time Super Bowl winner? "He's a hero of mine," I say.

She nods and stands up to leave. "And you're a hero of mine."

I smile. "I don't remember you saying that in high school."

She returns the smile. "If I knew then what I know now . . ."

Jenny leaves and I am once again alone with the documents. I start with the envelope that Sam left me a few days ago, which has remained unopened. It just didn't seem important.

I start with the copies of online stories about Elite, but none of it tells me anything I didn't already know. There is healthy skepticism in the press about Elite's prospects as a streaming service, but a willingness to back off and let them give it their best shot.

Once I am through with them, I check out the other thing that Sam sent. It's a rundown of everything that was on Larry

Hoffman's computer. He's right in that it shows Hoffman as being paranoid, worried among other things that his computer might have been attacked.

According to Sam, there is no evidence that the computer was compromised in any way, but Hoffman had extensively searched for information on the subject.

This fit exactly with what Pam Sparaco, his fiancée, had told me. In his last weeks he was afraid he was being watched, especially when they were in the Caymans. And he did not want her to use his computer, for fear she would accidentally download a virus.

But suddenly I realize that she was right when she told me the old joke, *Just because you're paranoid doesn't mean someone isn't really after you.* Somebody was after Larry Hoffman, and they killed him.

And I may know why he was suddenly so worried about maintaining the safety of his computer.

I call the number that Special Agent Haigler gave me, and it goes to voice mail. "I think I know what Miranov is doing," I say. "And you have to deal with it one way or the other by Monday. Call me back."

He will call me back, and I'll turn it over to him, and then it's out of my hands.

We get a tentative win to start Monday's court session.

Judge Slater has read our briefs regarding the admissibility of testimony regarding Bondar. Eddie Dowd, who on his worst day is better at writing briefs than I am on my best, did a terrific job on ours, and it has sort of paid off.

The judge's ruling is that she will allow the testimony, but will monitor it closely and rein us in if we go too far afield. It's a fair ruling, and one I am satisfied with.

What I am not satisfied with is the fact that I have not heard a word from Special Agent Haigler since our conversation two days ago. I don't know if I am right in what I told him, but I have to assume he at least followed up on it.

It would have been way too risky not to.

There has been no mention of it in the media either, though I don't think that proves anything either way. So all I can do is wait and hope; a good deal of our case depends on it.

"The defense calls Margaret Ambler."

Margaret Ambler is currently a security consultant to technology companies, and had worked as an assistant director in the Department of Homeland Security.

Eddie Dowd interviewed her yesterday and said she comes off as professional, serious, and very likable, not exactly a common combination. I have never spoken to her, so I hope his assessment is accurate.

I take her through her impressive credentials and ask her if she has ever heard of a man named Sergey Bondar.

"I certainly have."

"Did you hear of him in connection with your work at Homeland Security?"

"Yes."

"Are you free to speak about him here today?"

"If I weren't, I wouldn't be sitting here. I would never reveal classified information. Bondar is well-known."

"Please tell the jury about him."

"Well, for one thing, he has been wanted for murder by Interpol for almost two years. He is a Belarussian national, but his employer is known to be a Russian oligarch named Yaroslav Miranov."

"Is Miranov someone that Western governments admire?"

She smiles. "Only if they admire money laundering, arms dealing, cybercrime, and murder."

"And what does Bondar do for Miranov? Does he get his laundry, maybe act as his chauffeur? Does he do office work? Typing, collating?"

"Bondar does anything Miranov wants."

"Including murder?"

"Very definitely including murder."

"Thank you."

I turn the witness over to Shaffer, who frowns at having to deal with this nonsense. "Ms. Ambler, I'm sorry, but I was listening carefully to everything you had to say, and your record is very impressive, but . . . what are you doing here?"

She doesn't seem to understand the question, but says, "I was called here to be a witness."

"I understand and appreciate that," Shaffer says. "But what does any of this have to do with this trial?"

"I can't say."

Shaffer nods and smiles. "Join the club."

During the lunch break I check my phone for messages. There are none from Haigler, but one from Sam that is almost as good.

His message was, "Andy, I know you're in court, but I just wanted to call and say I told you so. A guy I know tried to sign up for that Elite streaming service, and he got a message saying they were having technical difficulties and that the launch was being delayed. I'm telling you, they are a train wreck waiting to happen."

Sam, you don't know this yet, but the wreck has already happened.

But I still want to hear from Haigler.

When court resumes I call Lawrence Gelman to the stand. He is a professor emeritus of telecommunications at Rutgers University. He has taught at Rutgers for almost thirty years, and is highly respected in the academic community. Now in his sixties and nearing retirement age, he has cut back on his teaching load, but has occasionally testified as an expert witness, usually in civil trials.

Once I give Professor Gelman the opportunity to describe his career accomplishments, I ask him if he has examined records the defense has subpoenaed and then provided to him. He confirms that he has examined them.

"Without getting into specifics yet, can you describe what those records are?"

"Yes, they are phone records related to a phone registered to a company in Belarus, in the name of Sergey Bondar."

"So they are phone calls that he made and received?"

"Yes, certainly. But there are also GPS records, obtained through cell towers, which show where his phone was at certain times."

"So there was a GPS in his phone?" I ask.

"Yes, that is true of virtually all smartphones."

"Let's start with the phone calls. Were there any calls between Mr. Bondar and Ryan Griffin?"

"Yes, a total of four. Three initiated by Mr. Griffin, one by Mr. Bondar."

"What was the last call between them?"

"Mr. Griffin made that call. It lasted for three minutes."

"When was this?"

"The night of his death."

"Were there any calls between Mr. Bondar and a man named Ruben Allegra?"

"Yes, there were six such calls."

"Thank you. Now let's talk about the GPS records. Are there any instances where Mr. Bondar was in Suffern, New York?"

"Yes."

"Do you know where in Suffern he was?"

"Yes. It appears to be an abandoned park . . . an area that is currently unused and uninhabited."

"Do the records show any other cell phones there at the same time?"

"Yes, one belonging to the same Mr. Ruben Allegra, and the other belonging to a Mr. Roger Gurley."

"Thank you. No further questions."

Shaffer's cross-examination is brief but devastating.

"Professor Gelman, you can tell us where Mr. Bondar's phone was, but can you tell us if he was carrying it?"

"No."

"So it's possible he wasn't even at these places, that someone else had his phone?"

"I couldn't say."

"Professor, in all the records the defense provided you regarding the location of Mr. Bondar's phone, were there any that showed it in the house where Mr. Griffin was murdered?"

"There were not."

"Thank you."

You were right," Special Agent Haigler says. He's reached me on my cell on the way home. "It was exactly the way you read it."

"So where does it stand now?"

"It's been taken down, and the relevant people are being questioned. Not sure who knew what yet, but we'll find out."

"Will it be announced to the public?"

"Yes, but not for a couple of days," he says. "Not until it all shakes out. But you did good."

"Now for the quid pro quo that I mentioned."

"I know. I'll be there to testify; I've already gotten approval internally," he says. "Not sure how much I'll be able to say yet, but it should be enough."

"Excellent. I'll be in touch on the specifics."

When I get home, I call Laurie and Jenny into the den. Laurie already knows what my theory was, but she doesn't know yet that it proved correct. Jenny has been in the dark about all of it.

"There's been a development with the new streaming service they call Elite."

"What is it?" Jenny asks.

"It's dead. It's never going to happen."

"Why?"

"Because the entire design of it was an enormous cybercrime. Once subscribers signed up and downloaded it, or downloaded a movie, then their computers and devices would have been immediately compromised."

"How?" Jenny asks.

"You know how you have to be careful not to click on a particular link or download something you're not sure of? Well, this was that on steroids. Anyone who signed up, including people who used the service on company computers, would have immediately been victimized by an invasive virus or malware. And they wouldn't know it until it was way too late.

"They would have been subjected to ransomware, loss of data, theft of crucial information. . . . The people running it could have made many billions of dollars and caused chaos and devastation."

"People running it?" Jenny asks. "You mean Arnold Chrisman and Audrey Dodge?"

"It remains to be seen what they knew or were involved in; that's being determined now. But the man pulling the strings was a Russian oligarch named Miranov. He has been using Ryan and his films to launder money all along."

"What effect will this have on our case?"

I knew she was going to ask that, and I wish I had a better answer. "I can't say for sure at this point. The first step will be to try to get Judge Slater to let us admit it."

"She might not?"

I nod. "It's a fifty-fifty call. But even then, our task will be to connect it to Griffin's death. We can certainly show that he, or at least his company, was connected to bad people, murderers.

"But what we haven't been able to do is find evidence that they killed Griffin, nor do we even know why they would have wanted to. He must have been a threat to them that they wanted to eliminate, but we don't know how or why."

"But we're in better shape than we were yesterday?" Jenny asks.

"We are."

Laurie speaks for the first time. "Is Haigler going to testify?"

I nod. "Yes, though what he'll be able to say will depend on Judge Slater."

"I can't believe Audrey was a part of this," Jenny says.

I don't want to tell her that I consider Audrey to be a suspect in the Griffin murder, at least not until I learn more. If she turns out to have been aware of what Miranov was doing, that would go a long way toward implicating her in the murder.

Audrey Dodge stood to profit from the death of Ryan Griffin; she took over his role in the company. She also had reason to seek revenge on him for cheating on her when they were married.

I don't know if Jenny will buy it, and I don't want to argue the point. Besides, I am far more concerned if Judge Slater will buy it. And if she does, then I have to sell it to the jury.

For now, I want to keep the focus on Bondar.

I am building the case against him point by point. So far I have identified him as a wanted murderer in Miranov's employ, and I have connected him through phone records to both Ryan Griffin and the security team.

I recall Janet Campbell to the stand. She's the waitress from Charlie's the night of the party, and I ask her to identify photographs of Danny and Gurley as the security guys who were with Griffin the night of the dinner party.

She does so, and next I call Todd Mauer, a homicide lieutenant with the Suffern Police Department. I show him the GPS map that Professor Gelman used to locate the abandoned park where the phones turned up that night.

"Lieutenant Stanton of Paterson PD told me that they had received a tip that there might be evidence of a crime at that site," he says.

"So you followed up on it?"

"Yes. With Lieutenant Stanton present as an observer."

"What did you find?"

"We found three victims, deceased and buried in recently dug graves. Each was shot once through the heart."

"Were you able to identify the victims?"

"Yes. Ruben Allegra, Roger Gurley, and Daniel Wilkins."

I show him photographs. "Are these photographs of the deceased?"

"They appear to be, yes."

"In your investigation, did you confirm that Mr. Gurley and Mr. Wilkins accompanied Ryan Griffin when he interrupted the dinner at Charlie's that Ms. Campbell testified about?"

"Yes."

"And was their partner in the security company Mr. Ruben Allegra?"

"Yes."

"Have you made an arrest for the three murders?"

"Yes. Sergey Bondar has been placed under arrest."

"Was your only evidence the fact that his phone was identified as having been at the scene?"

"No, there was significant forensic evidence tying him to the crime as well."

"Is he in your custody now?"

"No, the FBI has taken custody of him."

"Thank you."

Shaffer stands and continues the theme of his recent cross-examinations. "Lieutenant Mauer, did your investigation in any way connect Mr. Bondar to the murder of Ryan Griffin?"

"That was not our focus. Our investigation was properly limited to the crimes committed in our jurisdiction, which is Suffern, New York."

"So you know nothing about the murder of Mr. Griffin at all?"

"Only what I have seen in the media."

Shaffer actually sighs in weariness at having to tolerate and suffer through all this nonsense. "Thank you." His approach has been to disregard all this talk of Bondar as irrelevant, since none of it has related directly to the Griffin murder, which is the only reason we are all here in the first place.

Our next witness is Vince Sanders, who as a journalist is uncomfortable at having to be in this position. As a consumer of free food at Charlie's, he did not put up much of a fight when I said I needed him to be here.

I show Vince the initial story about Bondar that he wrote after meeting with me. "Did you write this story?"

"Yes."

"And it appeared in your newspaper?"

"Yes."

"Where did you get the information contained in the story?"

"From you," he says. "You called me and told me you had information about the Nichols case, and it was on the record."

I have him read parts of the story aloud, talking about Bondar, about his being wanted by Interpol, and about my belief that he was involved with the disappearance of the security guys. He also reads about my setting up a tip line and vowing to find Bondar and have him arrested.

Through the corner of my eye I can see Judge Slater frowning; she is still pissed that the story got published in the first place.

"Did I tell you why I was giving you the story?"

"Yes," Vince says. "But it was off the record."

I smile. "I release you from that obligation and it is now on the record. Please tell the jury."

"You wanted to bring Bondar out in the open. You wanted him to come after you."

"Thank you."

I expect Vince to say, *You're welcome, and I will officially never have to pay for another beer or burger for the duration of my natural life.*

Fortunately, he doesn't.

Media stories seem to break at different times these days. While I admit I never paid that much attention to it, it always seemed like news broke in time for the morning paper, or the late edition, or the network news.

Not anymore; now they seem to appear online at all hours. There seems to be a lessening of manipulation as to the timing of these things, or maybe I'm imagining it.

Sam calls a little after 7 P.M. to tell me that the story about Elite has exploded on the internet. We're just finishing dinner, so Laurie, Jenny, and I rush into the den to turn on the television. CNN is talking about it.

The Bureau announced the arrest of Arnold Chrisman in the scheme, which they described in some detail. It's basically what I told to Special Agent Haigler. The purpose was to get into the computers and devices of their customers.

Part of the genius of it was that they were appealing with their content to people with upscale tastes. They reasoned that it would therefore include wealthier people and those in jobs of some significance. Such people would make very lucrative targets.

The FBI didn't get into it, but it explains why Elite was entering a business with such great competition that they had only a small chance of success, and minimal profit potential.

Robby Divine had said he'd never consider investing in it; that the potential return just wasn't there. That didn't deter

Chrisman, or Miranov, because they weren't looking for a conventional return. They were investing in a cybercrime venture, not a streaming service.

The arrest apparently signals that Chrisman was in on it. I don't know if he would have fled once the operation was in full gear or not, because I don't know if Elite would have been identified as the source of the viruses, malware, and ransomware. That is above my technology pay grade.

Also arrested was James Richards, the guy who was heading up the tech division. He's the guy that Sam's chat-room friends said was a loser and incapable of setting up this kind of operation. Two other men in Richards's department have also been arrested.

But the Bureau made it clear that the technology area of the operation originated in Russia and was operating from there. They have identified exactly where it came from and who was behind it, though of course there is no chance the perpetrators will be extradited.

What bothers me is that Ryan Griffin is spoken about in the report, but is nowhere near the center of it. It is said that he had been a principal in the company when he was killed, and before the streaming service was announced.

Bondar is noticeably absent from the announcement. It's understandable; he really has nothing to do with the arrests that were made, and little to do with setting up the conspiracy. But the absence of Bondar in what the FBI has to say still bothers me.

Also absent from the Bureau's announcement, and apparently not among the arrested, is Audrey Dodge. That's not to say she won't be; they say that the investigation is ongoing. But for now she is off the hook.

The Bureau did not attempt to make a connection between Griffin's murder and this news; that will be up to me to attempt at trial. I don't mention it to Jenny, and I'll discuss it with Laurie later, but I have real doubts that Judge Slater will allow it in.

The sequestered jury is not going to hear about it if she doesn't.

And I know something in my gut—if the jury doesn't hear about it, we are dead.

The morning courtroom session is delayed when Shaffer asks for a meeting in the judge's chambers.

I know what it's about, and my feeling is confirmed by the presence of a court stenographer. Shaffer is going to try to cut the defense off at the knees, and he wants it in the record.

Judge Slater says, "Mr. Shaffer, you called this meeting."

"Yes, Your Honor. I would like to speak about the arrests the FBI made last night, breaking up the service called Elite. I assume you've seen the reports?"

"I have."

He nods. "Good. I am assuming that Mr. Carpenter plans to bring it all into the record . . . the entire alleged criminal enterprise, the money laundering, and the potential cybercrime."

"You assume correctly," I say.

"I would request that you issue a ruling on this, Your Honor. It is our position that it does not have the slightest relevance to our case. There has been no showing whatsoever that Mr. Griffin's death had any connection to his business dealings.

"The defense has not even established that Mr. Bondar had anything to do with the subject of this trial, though we have patiently watched him try to do so. But it is an entire three-thousand-mile leap to connect the business to it.

"Why would Mr. Griffin's death have helped the conspirators?

Can Mr. Carpenter explain that? This trial is not about money laundering, or cybercrime, or Russian oligarchs. It is about a stabbing death in a kitchen in Englewood Cliffs. If all of those things cannot be connected, tangibly connected, then this jury has no business hearing about it.

"It is far more prejudicial than probative, not even close."

It is a compelling argument; if this were a debate, I would wish to have Shaffer's position to argue.

"Mr. Carpenter?"

"Your Honor, it may not surprise you to learn that I could not disagree more with Mr. Shaffer. Mr. Griffin was in the middle; he was a centerpiece in a world that we now know was a cesspool of crime. Crime and murder.

"We don't know why they eliminated Griffin; maybe someday we will. But it is not necessary that we have every answer before we pose a question. We also don't know why Bondar killed the security guards, but we know that he did.

"There is another murder, that of Larry Hoffman, that was closely associated with Mr. Griffin. We haven't yet introduced that in court because we cannot tie it to Bondar. But we can bring in testimony about it, and that will drive the point home even more.

"Mr. Griffin was involved with killers; he was in a high-stakes world of international criminals who would obviously do anything to further their conspiracy. To say that the jury does not have a right to consider that, to say that it might give them pause and create reasonable doubt, defies logic.

"We are searching for the truth, and in the service of that we need to give the jury all the facts that we can. What the FBI announced yesterday are facts, and they relate directly to this case.

"With respect, the jury needs to hear it all."

We kick it around awhile longer, but the arguments do not change. Judge Slater says that she will ponder the matter and make her decision later today, and we head back into court.

To use a technical legal term, I think we are in deep shit.

Pete Stanton is our next witness. He has testified in a defense case before, but as a cop he's never thrilled about it.

"Captain Stanton, were you called to my house in Paterson?"

"Yes."

"If you know, was this after the story about Bondar ran in the local paper?"

"Yes, I believe it was three days later."

"And are you aware of testimony by Vince Sanders that the purpose of the story was to tie Mr. Bondar to this case? And to get him to come after me?"

"Yes, I am aware of that testimony."

"What did you find when you got to my house?"

"You were in the backyard with two of your investigators, Laurie Collins and Marcus Clark. And Mr. Bondar was there as well."

"What was Mr. Bondar doing?"

"He was not doing anything; he was unconscious. He had a physical confrontation with Mr. Clark, and it did not go well for him."

"Was his handgun there?"

"Yes, he had been disarmed."

"What were the circumstances that had taken place, as they were related to you by the witnesses?" I ask.

"You had expected him to come after you, based on the article, so Mr. Clark and Ms. Collins planned to intercept him if he did so. He did, and they did."

"Did you take him into custody?"

"Briefly."

"Why briefly?"

"The crime he was charged with was attempted breaking and entering. He was already wanted in Suffern for multiple murders, so those charges took precedence, and we turned him over to Suffern PD. They in turn gave him to federal law enforcement."

"When you talk about the murders in Suffern, are you referring to the three security guards, two of whom were assigned to protect Mr. Griffin?" I'm beating this to death, but I want to make sure the jury cannot miss the connection.

"Yes."

Shaffer's cross to Pete is typically brief. "Lieutenant Stanton, in your investigation of this matter, did you find any connection between Mr. Bondar and Ryan Griffin's death?"

"I did not, but I was not searching for it. That's not my case."

"Are you aware of any such connection being made by any other law enforcement organization?"

"I am not, but I don't get briefed by other law enforcement organizations."

"I understand. No further questions."

During lunch I assess where we are and how we can go forward. If Judge Slater allows testimony about Griffin Entertainment and Elite, we obviously have a bunch of paths to take and witnesses to call.

If she does not, we might be done. I don't want to call the Bronx police officer who could testify to Griffin's connection to the drug dealer. There is no indication that drugs had anything to do with the murder, and for me to point to it shows weakness.

I can't spend an entire trial saying Bondar did it, and then say, *But if he didn't, then the drug dealer did.*

I also don't want to call Linda Ivers; we're too far along for character witnesses. One way or another, the die is cast. So if Judge Slater turns us down on Griffin Entertainment and Elite, we're done.

When I get back to court, the judge calls Shaffer and me back to her chambers. She gets right to the point. "I've decided that the business evidence is not directly relevant and shall not be introduced in this trial."

We're done.

n case we lose, I am going to have Eddie Dowd start working on an appeal now.

I don't think we'd prevail, but it would certainly be worth a shot. Judge Slater could have gone either way on the admissibility of the business stuff, which is why an appeal is unlikely to be successful. It's a very close call, and therefore reasonable.

Before court resumes, I call Special Agent Haigler to tell him he won't have to testify. "Can you still win the case?" he asks.

"We have a puncher's chance."

"Well, I'm rooting for you," he says. "You really saved our ass."

"Always glad to help. Anything new on the case?"

"Bondar copped to the Suffern killings and also Larry Hoffman. He won't give up Miranov even though we'd never get to him anyway."

"What about Griffin? Any change on that front?"

"Still denies it; if that changes you'll be the first call I make."

"I can use it. What about Audrey Dodge?"

"He says she wasn't a part of it."

"You believe him?"

"Probably, but not because he has any relationship with the truth at all. It's more because he has nothing to gain by shielding her, once he's admitted to all this other stuff."

The first thing I say when we return to open court is, "The

defense rests, Your Honor." I can feel Jenny tense up beside me; she was expecting that we'd be calling witnesses about the business.

Judge Slater asks if we are ready to give closing statements, and Shaffer and I both say that we are.

Shaffer stands and walks toward the jury. Like me, he does not use a podium. "Ladies and gentleman, we've just met, so we really haven't gotten to know each other. People who do know me, my family and close friends, know I am awful at predicting things.

"I predict an NBA championship for the Knicks every year, and if I predict a stock is going to go up, you should sell it immediately. It's been like that for as long as I can remember.

"But this time I am happy to say I know I got it right. I stood here at the beginning of the trial, and I know that feels like a long time ago, and I predicted what would happen. I told you that we would present proof, beyond a reasonable doubt, that Jenny Nichols killed Ryan Griffin, in cold blood with a knife in his back.

"I also told you that the defense would spin a story that had nothing to do with Mr. Griffin's murder, in an attempt to distract you. I told you that Mr. Carpenter was a good storyteller, and he proved me right.

"You sat through witness after witness talking about a man named Sergey Bondar, who we agree is a criminal and a murderer. But was there any evidence tying him to Mr. Griffin's death? None. Zero.

"You saw voluminous phone records; we learned where Mr. Bondar, or at least his phone, was in significant detail. But let me ask you . . . did those records show his phone at the house in Englewood Cliffs that night? If they did, don't you think you would have heard about it?

"The reason you didn't is that Bondar wasn't there, and he didn't kill Ryan Griffin. Jenny Nichols did, in her kitchen, with her cake knife.

"Maybe Ryan Griffin behaved badly toward her. Maybe he cheated on her, maybe he verbally abused her. None of that, even if it happened, gave her the right to put a knife in Ryan Griffin's back when he turned away from her.

"I'm going to make some final predictions. I'm going to predict that you are going to listen to Mr. Carpenter and then the judge's instruction. Then I predict that you are going to deliberate and look at the facts and evidence clearly and dispassionately.

"Then I predict that you are going to do your job and convict Jenny Nichols of murder. Thank you for listening and for your service to this community."

I get up to give my closing statement without showing the pessimism that I feel.

"Ladies and gentleman, Mr. Shaffer is right about one thing; I did spend the last few days telling you a story. What he does not understand, or at least won't tell you, is that the story is nonfiction.

"Every word is true.

"Ryan Griffin was in phone contact with a multiple murderer, an international wanted criminal named Sergey Bondar. We know that among Bondar's crimes were the murders of the three men assigned to protect Mr. Griffin.

"That is true.

"When I put out the word publicly that Mr. Bondar was a person of interest in this case, and asked for the public's help in finding him, he came to my house and tried to kill me.

"That is true.

"Does all of this not seem strange to you? Does it not cause you to wonder what was going on? Ryan Griffin was surrounded by murder, and he was murdered himself. Jenny Nichols is not accused of burying three security guards in Suffern, New York, and she should not be accused of killing a man in Englewood Cliffs, New Jersey.

"So here is the situation you have to ponder. On the one hand, you have Jenny Nichols, a young woman who has never committed an act of any kind of violence in her life. Who has never been accused of any crime whatsoever.

"And you have Sergey Bondar, a multiple murderer who was in contact with the victim, and who killed his security guards.

"These facts, this true story, must give you reasonable doubt as to Ms. Nichols's guilt. You must consider it at the very least possible that Sergey Bondar committed this crime. And if you do, you must find Jenny Nichols not guilty, and give her her life back.

"Thank you for your service. Like Mr. Shaffer, I deeply appreciate it."

There is absolutely nothing worse than waiting for a verdict, and this time is worse than usual.

Even though I am always pessimistic, this time I truly believe we are going to lose. It fills me with a sense of dread that is overwhelming and inescapable.

The other thing that makes it so much more awful than past cases is that the real loser, the person whose life of freedom will come to a permanent end, is living in our house.

I know that she is tortured and panicked, and I want to make her feel better, but I can't without lying. So instead I mutter inanities like, "You never know," and "Juries are impossible to predict." They don't make her feel any better.

It's been two days now since the jury went off to deliberate. I guess on some level that encourages me; at least the jury didn't consider it a slam dunk against us. But every minute that we wait feels like an hour.

Jenny and Laurie have been gardening like crazy; with the work they are putting in, we will have enough vegetables to feed Venezuela. Linda Ivers came over again yesterday to lend moral support, but she was way too upbeat. If Jenny was to take what Linda said at face value, she'd already be booking a flight back to Los Angeles.

Eddie Dowd has emailed me a copy of our appeals brief and

he's done a great job. I had just a few edits, and now it's ready to go. I just hope we don't need it.

Every time the phone rings I think I'm going to pass out; I'm not handling this well at all. It's just rung, and Laurie has gotten it in the other room.

She comes in a few moments later. "They want you down there. They have a verdict."

Five minutes later the bailiffs arrive to escort Jenny to court. I see her pick up Mamie and give her a hug. She knows she may not see her again. It is one of the saddest things I have ever seen.

It is even more of a madhouse than usual in the streets near the courthouse. The word of a verdict has spread like wildfire. I see media reporters standing on the courthouse steps in front of their camera operators, waiting to breathlessly report the verdict when they hear it.

Eddie Dowd is already at the defense table when I get there. I know he shares my pessimism but neither of us voices it right now. It doesn't matter what we think. The decision has been made . . . it's out of our hands.

Shaffer comes over to congratulate me on a good battle, no matter how it ends. I shake his hand, but even though I know he was just doing his job, what I really would like to do is wring his neck.

Jenny is brought in; I know she's dying inside, but she's trying not to show it. She sits down and becomes one of the few defendants in this pre-verdict moment not to ask what I think. She knows what I think.

Judge Slater comes in and then calls for the jury. The gallery is packed but deathly silent. That won't last for long.

"Have you reached a verdict?"

"We have, Your Honor," says the foreman.

The bailiff goes to retrieve it and brings it to the judge, who reads it silently. He then takes it back and gives it to the court clerk, and Judge Slater instructs her to read it, after first telling Jenny to stand.

Jenny, Eddie, and I rise as one. My arm is around Jenny's waist in a gesture of support, or a way to keep my legs from collapsing under me.

"We the jury, in the case of New Jersey versus Jennifer Nichols, as to count one, the homicide of Mr. Ryan Griffin, find the defendant, Jennifer Nichols, guilty of the crime of first-degree homicide."

The gallery explodes and the judge's gavel is not sufficient to get them quiet. Jenny puts her head down; I can't imagine what is going through her mind.

She turns to me and all I can say is, "I'm sorry. But it's not over."

"It feels over," she says. "You did all you could, and you were wonderful, but it's over."

Then she adds, "Please take care of Mamie."

know I said there is nothing worse than waiting for a verdict, and I believed it at the time, but it was total horseshit.

The absolute worst thing is losing a verdict and knowing that your client is going to go to jail for something they didn't do. And knowing, knowing with certainty, that the reason they lost is because their lawyer is a loser.

If Jenny is innocent, then the real-world facts were in her favor. Her lawyer failed to uncover those facts, and couldn't get the jury to see the truth.

But will the lawyer suffer for it? No, the lawyer goes free.

Next case.

I don't know what to do with myself or how to deal with this feeling. It is why I will never try another goddamn case again. The last thing I will do as an attorney is file an appeal for Jenny, and while she rots in jail the appeals court will consider it, and then they will turn it down.

I know Laurie is feeling for Jenny, and for me, but I can't allow her to make me feel better. I need to feel this pain, and process it, because I deserve it.

It's been three days since the verdict. I've visited Jenny twice, and I've talked about the appeal, but neither of us has any confidence. Her sentencing is scheduled for six weeks down the road, and that will be another truly awful day when it arrives. And every day after that will be just as bad.

I've only been out of the house to walk the dogs. Even Tara has not been able to comfort me, try as she might. I am well beyond comforting.

Laurie has suggested the last two nights that I go to Charlie's and sit and watch sports with Vince and Pete. She thinks that a night spent with my friends insulting each other might make me feel better, but I have no interest in going.

I've given in tonight and I'm going with Laurie to a diner on Route 4 for a quick dinner. I don't want to go, but I don't want to be home either. I don't want to be anywhere.

Once we're finished eating, we order coffee. Laurie says, "Andy, I know it's easy for me to say, but you have to snap out of this. You did your best; no one could have done better."

"Somebody could have won."

"Andy, listen to me . . ." she says, putting her hand on mine on the table. Just then her cell phone rings, and she says, "Damn . . . one second, I'm going to shut this thing off."

She shuts her phone off and turns back to me, but I'm too busy thinking and realizing. My mind is racing, not listening. "Andy, what I was going to say was . . ."

"Hold the thought, Laurie. Right now we have to get out of here."

"Why?"

"Because I understand everything now."

Audrey Dodge killed Ryan Griffin," I say to Linda Ivers when I call her.

"She did? How do you know that?"

"It has to do with something you told me, about overhearing them having an argument in the office."

"I don't understand."

"Come over tomorrow morning at eleven and I'll explain everything. I'm going to need your help."

"I'll do anything for Jenny, you know that."

With that accomplished, I call Sam. "Sam, I need you to access the guest records of the Warwick Hotel on Fifty-fourth Street, and I need you to set something else up for me."

"Roger that; what do you need?"

I don't even take the time to mock Sam's use of the word *roger*; there's no time for that. Instead I have to call Pete Stanton and convince him to do something for me. I will be using the promise of a lifetime of free food and beer in my pitch.

If Jenny were here, I could ask her the question that would tell me if I am right or wrong, but she's not, so I'm just going to move ahead.

If I'm wrong, I can go back to being miserable.

Tara comes over to me for a snuggle, her tail wagging. I think she could tell I'm feeling hopeful, if not upbeat.

"Tara, this just might work out."

"ell me again about the argument between Griffin and Audrey Dodge." Linda Ivers and I are sitting in the den and talking.

"I've been thinking about it for a long time, and especially since you called last night," she says. "But I don't remember any more than I told you. It seemed like it was about business, but then it got personal. Ryan laughed at her, and then she said she could kill him. I remember that very clearly."

Before I can answer, I hear Laurie come in the front door. She comes to the door of the den, looks in, and nods at me. Then she leaves.

"You said it happened a day or two before the murder. Could you have been wrong? Could it have been the same day?"

She thinks for a moment. "No, I don't think so. Maybe . . . it was such a terrible time; maybe I'm getting it wrong."

"Were you in the office the day of the murder? Did you see Audrey?"

"I wasn't there."

"Did you see Ryan that day?"

"No, but I wouldn't have, because I wasn't in the office or on the set. Why do you think Audrey did it?"

I ignore the question and say, "Here is the only question I have, and only you can answer it for me. Why did you kill Ryan Griffin?"

She physically recoils, stunned, giving new meaning to the phrase *taken aback*. I can see panic in her face as she tries to figure out the best answer, but all she can come up with is, "What do you mean? Is that a joke?"

"Definitely not, Linda, and you should take it very seriously. You were her assistant; she needed to be able to reach you. So she got you a phone to use; maybe she paid for it, or maybe the production did. But this way you wouldn't have to pay the bill; it could be written off by Jenny or the production."

"So?"

"So there were two phones in Jenny's name, hers and yours. When we found out through the phone records that Jenny's phone was there at the house that night, it was really yours, but in her name."

"This is crazy; it had to be hers. I wasn't there."

"She turned her phone off at the party when Griffin called her twice. It was your phone, Linda."

"I went to sleep early that night at the hotel."

"Wrong again. You were staying at the Warwick. We have security footage of you leaving the hotel and arriving back much later. And we have E-ZPass records of your rental car crossing the bridge."

I'm lying about both of those things, but Laurie had just gone outside to confirm that Linda's car had an E-ZPass device.

I can see the panic registering on her face. "Andy . . ."

"Griffin called the Warwick Hotel that night; that's where you were staying. Maybe he asked you where Jenny was staying because he wanted to go there. You told him, but you met him there."

"No . . ."

"Why, Linda? He was rumored to be having an affair with someone on the production. Was that you? Did he reject you?"

"No . . ."

"It's over, Linda. I can prove it all."

She's quiet for a few moments, processing this . . . probably trying to figure a way out. Then, "He told me he loved me, but he was lying. He wanted Jenny; he was obsessed with Jenny. She had everything, and she didn't even want him. I wanted him!

"He laughed at me that night. He didn't laugh at Audrey like I said; he laughed at me. Then he turned his back on me. I was pleading with him, and he turned his back."

"You didn't have to kill him."

"I didn't plan to. I couldn't stand it, and I picked up the knife. I just did it."

Pete Stanton and three officers walk into the room. They take Linda by the arms and bring her to her feet, then cuff her hands behind her back. Pete reads her Miranda rights and arrests her.

Sam Willis walks into the room with two discs. "It's all recorded on here, and I have a copy for you, Pete." He hands one disc to Pete and one to me.

"I'll make good use of it," I say.

played the tape for Judge Slater and Shaffer at the same time, and they really stepped up.

Pete Stanton was there as well, verifying everything that I said and that the tape showed. Judge Slater and Shaffer immediately understood what they were seeing and hearing, and it is to their everlasting credit that they knew what had to be done.

They just didn't know how to do it, and neither did I. It actually became a session in which the defense, prosecution, and judge tossed around ideas about how best to get the just-convicted murderer out of jail the fastest.

It was one of the weirder meetings I have ever been in.

Shaffer was the one who came up with the best plan. He said that the defense should file a motion for a new trial. The prosecution would join in that motion, and it would be filed with Judge Slater.

The judge would quickly grant the motion, and that would put the prosecution in a position where they could dismiss the charges, avoiding the trial. That would leave Jenny free and with the conviction wiped from her record.

I called Eddie Dowd and told him what was needed, and we reconvene in the judge's chambers an hour and a half later. The motion is written perfectly, as I knew it would be.

Shaffer signs his name to it, and we move into open court. It is the first time in this courtroom without a packed gallery, so it seems strange. Everything about this situation is strange.

Jenny is brought in, still wearing prison clothing. I realize that she is the only person in the room who has no idea what is happening. She looks completely confused, and I don't blame her.

"What is going on, Andy?"

Judge Slater enters and takes her seat, so there is no time for me to tell Jenny anything. "Just sit back and enjoy the show," I say.

Judge Slater makes sure we are on the record and says, "The court has a defense motion for a new trial based on newly uncovered evidence. The prosecution has signed on to the motion, and it is hereby granted."

Jenny leans over to me and whispers, "A new trial?"

I hold up my hand in a gesture telling her to wait.

"Your Honor, the prosecution has another motion."

"What is it?"

"We move to dismiss all charges, with prejudice."

The judge slams her gavel. "Granted. Ms. Nichols, you are free to go. I am personally sorry you had to go through this."

Jenny looks like she has been struck by a bolt of lightning. "Andy, does this mean what I think it does?"

"It means exactly what you think it does. Get some decent clothes on; I don't want Mamie to see you dressed like that."

We almost always have victory parties at Charlie's, in the upstairs room.

But it has never been more appropriate than this time, since this is where it all began.

Of course, we didn't technically have a victory during the trial; the jury screwed that up by using the word *guilty*. But it definitely worked out.

Everybody who was at the original dinner is here, plus Pete Stanton and Eddie Dowd. Mamie has also made a return appearance. Tara and the crew are at home keeping Ricky company as he plays video games with his friends from the tour.

Vince has been hounding me with questions because he wants to write follow-up exclusive stories. He apparently likes being on CNN. In a shocking development that foretells the end of our society, *Vince Sanders* was trending the other day on Twitter.

He asks me how I knew it was Linda Ivers.

I've already told him about the two phones being in Jenny's name, and Jenny having turned her phone off at the party. I add, "When Linda was over at the house recently, she got a call from Edward Markle that was meant for Jenny. He must have read the phone number off the production list, and Linda's phone was in Jenny's name."

I add, "We knew that Griffin called the Warwick that night. Once I confirmed that Linda stayed there, I was pretty sure I was right. Plus, Gurley told me that he had seen a woman at the house when they dropped Griffin off.

"Linda had been at the house, so she would have known that Jenny sometimes forgot to lock up, and often left windows open. And the director of the film told me there were rumors that Griffin was having an affair with someone connected to the production.

"So I finally put it all together. I could have been wrong; I'm just glad I wasn't."

Jenny has overheard us and joins the conversation. She asks, "What about the streaming service? How did you know it was one big cybercrime?"

"Again, I wasn't positive, but it fit. Larry Hoffman was paranoid about someone invading his computer just before he died. He must have found out what was really going on.

"And the company did not make business sense. Sam said the guys they hired could not pull it off, and they would have needed a fortune to make a go of it. This way they didn't need to spend the fortune on content, because all they cared about was penetrating the computers of subscribers.

Once they had an initial wave, they had achieved their goal. With Miranov having a record of cybercrime, it just all fit. But again, I wasn't positive, and I could have been wrong."

"Anything else?" Vince asks.

I put my arm around Jenny. "One more thing. Did you know we dated in high school?"

Jenny smiles. "You can print it. I want everybody to know."